THE MAN WITH THE
MACKINTOSH
OVERCOAT

Table Of Contents

Chapter 1

I won't be a Billionaire for long. I'm going to give most of the money away and I'm going to do it anonymously. All the big lotteries worldwide combined to create a Mega Millions Lottery with a massive jackpot of one Billion Euro. The media worldwide went into a frenzy when it was announced that there was only one winning ticket. Then, when it was announced that the winning ticket was sold in Ireland, we were all in a frenzy. Well, I wasn't, the country was.

I didn't check my ticket then because I never check these things until I have to, or until the game is up. I always thought that if I don't check it, then I still have a chance. I can still dream. How many times have you been told there was a lottery jackpot winner? You check your ticket, get the usual message; 'Not A Winner,' then crumple it and throw it in the bin along with your dreams. If I don't check my ticket, it's not a losing ticket yet. I checked my ticket yesterday, let me tell you; Dreams can come through.

I hadn't intended on checking my ticket. I had just arrived home and was parked in my driveway. I had my lottery ticket in my shirt pocket, felt like it was burning a hole in there all day. It was my ticket, it's just that I had sort of lost it.

Mrs Fogarty, the nosey neighbour, or one of the nosey neighbours, was across the road when I got home. She was pretending to look busy in her front garden, but I knew she was waiting for me to get out of the car, so she could mooch over for some gossip. Two can play that game, so I waited in my car and pretended I was busy on my phone. I checked for any missed calls. Truth is, I had been busy checking my phone like a teenager all day, hoping for a call from Claire.

Mrs Fogarty was a great friend of my mother, so I try to give her a bit of leeway if I can, for my Mother's sake. I just wasn't in the mood for her yesterday. If I'm honest, I wasn't ready for her, really. I knew fine well what gossip she was after.

Maybe I should explain a few things. My name is Billy; I'm a taxi driver in Dublin. I'm engaged to Claire, at least, I think we're still engaged. I'm not really sure where I stand with her at the moment. I have a fantastic sixteen-year-old daughter from a previous relationship, her name is Jane. I cherish any time I get to spend with her.

Claire and I have had a rough time lately. We were supposed to get married last year. Everything was booked, family was all due to fly home and then boom; We had a lockdown because of Covid. One week before our wedding, the entire country, the entire world, really; everything shut down because of Covid. It was devastating for us, for everyone.

Claire moved out last week. She moved back to her parent's house. Claire said she needs time to think and to get her head straight. She even suggested maybe things happened for a reason last year, maybe we were not supposed to get married after all. She only said maybe, so still a chance then, or wishful thinking on my part.

I wasn't too worried initially. We did have a row before. Claire moved out for a couple of days, but we sorted it all out. This has been going on for a week, so I'm more than a bit worried now.

The situation with her has been constantly on my mind. We've had the odd brief phone call, and we did meet for a chat. If I'm honest, all this business with her has knocked me back; knocked the stuffing out of me. I've realised that maybe I was just taking things for granted between us. Claire said I was dragging my feet on booking a new wedding date, but, in my defence, that was only because of the whole uncertainty of everything around Covid.

I found my lottery ticket in my bin yesterday morning! Yes, in the bin! Claire called around to the house for our chat the previous evening. I had given the house a quick tidy and put a bottle of her favourite wine in the fridge. She didn't stay for a glass of wine, but the 'chat' went well, or let's just say it could have gone worse. In fact, I kind of felt Claire was softening her stance a little.

She was still wearing her engagement ring, so I'm more than hopeful we will sort things out. She said she'd phone me, which is why I was constantly checking my phone yesterday. I couldn't let that bottle of wine go to waste, so I kind of had a glass or three after she left.

I regretted having the wine because I had an early start yesterday, a pickup at the airport. It was bin collection day, and the bin was at the top of my driveway. As I reversed my taxi out, I knocked the bin over. No damage done, but it caused a bit of a stir; a few of the neighbours were at their windows having a gawk, to see what was going on, or really to make sure I hadn't damaged their property.

I scrambled out of my taxi, fixed the bin upright, picked up what had fallen out and there it was, my lottery ticket.

Somehow, probably when I was tidying the house before Claire arrived, I must have put my lottery ticket in the bin. I stuffed it in my shirt pocket, hence the burning feeling I had been having there all day. Of course, it could have been burning, because maybe Claire is going to break my heart.

While I was waiting in my car for Mrs Fogarty to go, it was announced on the car radio that the winning ticket was sold in the shop where I had, in fact, bought my ticket. I fumbled to get the ticket out of my shirt pocket and just caught the last two numbers as they were called out. I didn't have those numbers on my first line, but I already knew that. I had picked numbers based around Jane and Claire's birthdays, and the date my Mother passed away. The ticket had two lines; my other line was a random selection. I had those two numbers, so I figured I had a bit of a chance. It was time to check my ticket.

I checked my car mirrors and had a quick look over my shoulder. I couldn't see Mrs Fogarty. I figured she had got fed up waiting and went back into her house. I got out of the car and made a run for my front door, but just before I got there; "Ah, there you are now, Billy. How are things?" She had ambushed me.

"I'm great, Mrs Fogarty. Happy new year to you, and to Mr Fogarty. How are you both getting on?" She had a quick look in the car and glanced in the front window of the house, as if she was looking for someone.

"How is Claire keeping? I haven't seen her for a while."

"Claire is great, Mrs Fogarty. She's…. She's minding her mother for a few days." I lied. 'Wish you'd mind your own business,' I said, not out loud, in my head. "I'll tell Claire you were asking for her." We exchanged a bit of small talk before I managed to escape and get into the house.

I Googled for the winning numbers on my phone; And there they were, my numbers. I had all eight numbers. Had I won the Lottery? Not only that, the Mega Millions Lottery. Had I won a Billion Euro? I turned on the television and found a news channel. They had been calling out the winning numbers on the news almost nonstop in the last few days. Do you think they called them out now? No, instead we had talk about how the winner has not claimed the jackpot yet. That they are losing thousands of Euro every day in interest. I got impatient and shouted at the television. "I know all of this. What are the winning numbers so I can check my ticket?"

I Googled for the winning numbers again, but just as the numbers popped up on my screen, my phone rang, which frightened the bejasus out of me. It was Claire. I got such a fright and was so flustered that I was probably a bit hasty with her, rude even. I was keen to check my ticket, and the numbers were then being called out on the television, too.

I had been waiting and hoping for that phone call all day, but I can't recall much of the conversation. All I remember is Claire saying, "You're not even listening, Billy. If you're too busy or have something better to do, fine." …. and she hung up.

It was the same numbers every time, my numbers. My first instinct was to phone Claire back. No, wait, I needed to make sure. I needed to verify this officially before I told Claire, before I told anyone. I went to Google again. How much is a Billion Euro? I didn't actually know.

One Billion is one thousand million. Had I won a thousand million Euro? I tried to stay calm. 'You need to think straight, Billy,' I told myself. I decided to drive to my local shop. They have one of those ticket checkers there where I could scan my ticket without going to the service counter. That would confirm it, or not, of course.

I looked up and down the street to make sure the coast was clear, or make sure Mrs Fogarty was gone, at least. I jumped in the car. 'Stay calm Billy,' I kept telling myself. I reversed the car out. Bang, I hit my bin again. It was empty now, but neighbours were back at their windows again. I jumped out of the car and clumsily fixed the bin while apologetically waving at the neighbours.

I felt like everyone was watching me when I went into the shop. They weren't. People were just getting on with their own business. The ticket checker was located near the entrance to the shop. Perfect, it was possible for me to check the ticket discreetly and then leave; the other customers would barely notice I was there.

Except, you know who, was there, minding everyone's business. She was at the service counter chatting to Mr Murphy, the shop owner. It didn't take her long to spot me at the door. "Ah, there you are again, Billy," and jokingly, "You must be following me." I grabbed a shopping basket.

"Mrs Fogarty, good to see you again, and good to see you too, Mr Murphy. Nice evening, isn't it?" I put a few random items in my basket and edged myself closer to the ticket checker. I was shaking with fear and anticipation. A few people left the shop. Mrs Fogarty and Mr Murphy were the only other people in the shop now. They were engrossed in conversation, so I decided to go for it.

I was just about to check my ticket, but then I changed my mind. I suddenly had visions of Las Vegas. You know, when they hit the jackpot on one of those slot machines and all hell breaks loose. Bells, whistles, and confetti everywhere. Or a loudspeaker on for everyone to hear. 'Jackpot! We have the Billion Euro jackpot winner here.'

I was pausing by the checker, my lottery ticket in my hand, my hand shaking; wondering what would happen if I scanned the ticket. "I can check that for you over here Billy, give it here. That machine there can be moody." It was Mr Murphy, his hand outstretched at the counter. There was an uncomfortable pause as I stood there.

"You're okay, Mr Murphy, I checked it. No luck. Not me this time, anyway." Off I went, out the door. I pretended to throw my lottery ticket in the bin on my way out. I folded it and put it back in my pocket. I felt like a fugitive. Ireland's most wanted. In fact, the world's most wanted. I figured I could phone the Lottery next morning. They'd confirm it for me, or not, of course.

As I was walking to my car, Mr Murphy shouted after me, "Billy, Billy." Shit, I was thinking, he knows. He's on to me. How does he know? "Billy, did you forget something?" My immediate reaction was to check my pocket for my lottery ticket. Then I realised I still had my shopping basket under my arm. I hadn't paid for my stuff.

"Shit, sorry Mr Murphy." I went back into the shop. I went to the counter and paid for my shopping. I hadn't paid attention to what I put in my basket. There was bleach, sanitary towels, a ball of string and a cabbage. "Sorry Mr Murphy, my head's all over the place lately." He put me at ease.

"Ah, no problem, Billy. Happens to us all."

"Sorry again," I said, and then meekly walked out of the shop. Mrs Fogarty whispered to Mr Murphy as I left.

"Claire has moved out, gone to stay with her Mother, apparently." Wink, wink, nudge, nudge.

I was thinking of downloading the lottery app on my phone. I could check my ticket on that. I thought better of it. They'd have my number and who knows what other information they'd have from my phone. I decided to wait and phone them in the morning.

I checked the ticket over and over before I went to bed. I hardly slept all night. I was imagining how I could spend this, who I would give money to. Then reminding myself that the ticket had to be officially verified before I could make any plans. I also told myself that if this ticket is in fact the winning ticket, then I have to stay anonymous.

I put the ticket under my mattress. I barely slept a wink; my mind was racing. I jumped out of bed in the middle of the night. Had I checked the date on the ticket? Maybe I had the right numbers, but on the wrong date. I had checked the date several times. Got up and checked again. Just in case.

Where do you keep a ticket worth a Billion…. or that might be worth a Billion Euro? It's safe under my mattress when I'm asleep on it. What about during the day? Do you keep it in your wallet? Might get pick-pocketed or lose it. Do I hide it in the house? What if the house gets burgled? I was thinking about the attic. I could hide it up there. What if there's a fire, and the house gets burned down? And to think, the ticket nearly went out with the bin yesterday.

I hid it in my shed. At the back, under all the clutter. Then I had visions of it being eaten by mice. I got the ticket out of the shed again. Could I leave it in the Bank for safe keeping? They could put it in their safe. Someone in the bank would tell. Someone always tells, secrets always get told.

I was so flustered; my hands were sweating, and I was thinking the ticket might get damaged if I kept handling it. I decided on the shed, but I sealed it in an old jam jar, mouse proof! I put it in a box at the back under all the clutter; I added more clutter on top. I locked the shed.

I was even thinking if there was a fire in the shed, there's a good chance the ticket will be okay in that jam jar. Amazing the things you think of when you can't think straight.

I was spending and giving away all this money in my head, and my head was spinning. The media circus around the Billion Euro ticket was massive. It still is, not just in Ireland; This was world news. I decided to stay anonymous no matter what. None of my family will ever have to work again. I don't know though, is that a good thing?

I had visions of Brad, my eighteen-year-old nephew in Chicago, crashing his Lamborghini sports car at one hundred miles an hour. It's my fault for giving him too much money. Or my daughter Jane deciding not to follow her dreams of becoming a vet. Living the easy life with low-life friends instead.

I needed to calm myself down. I was wishing Claire was with me, wishing things were better between us. Claire would know what to do; she'd keep me calm and grounded. I wanted to phone her, but no, not as things are. Not until the ticket had been verified.

It was time to phone the Lottery and verify my ticket. I got my ticket and was ready to dial. I was so nervous about them finding out my name. I even decided on using the landline. For some illogical reason, I thought it might be more secure.

I dialled the number. Ticket in my hand and my hand was shaking uncontrollably. I reminded myself to stay calm. 'Stay calm, Billy, and stay anonymous.' I imagined there was someone waiting by a special red phone in the Lottery head office. Waiting for the Billion Euro ticket winner to call. The entire world was waiting for me to call.

After about four rings, the phone was answered. It was an automated service. The voice had an American accent. I had the phone wedged between my shoulder and my ear because I needed one hand to keep my other hand steady holding my ticket.

'Welcome to the National Lottery. Please be advised that calls may be recorded and monitored for training and quality purposes. Please select one of the following options.' I hung up the phone.

I got unsettled by the 'calls may be recorded' bit. And what if they can trace my call? 'That's normal, Billy,' I told myself, nothing unusual going on, and why would they trace my call? I dialled the number again and waited for my automated American friend to give me the options.

'If you are a member of the public and would like to speak to a National Lottery advisor, press one. If you are a member of the public and would like to speak with a member of our claims team, press two. If you're a retail agent and would like to place an order, press three. If you are'.... I pressed number two on the phone.

It was still automated, but with an Irish accent this time. 'Thank you for phoning the National Lottery. A member of our claims team will be with you shortly.' A bit of soft music while I was on hold. Felt like I was on hold for an age, but it was only a few seconds. Both of my hands were shaking now.

It was another Irish accent that greeted me, a real person this time. "Hello, National Lottery claims team. How can I help you today?" I was so flustered I almost gave my name straight away.

"Hi, my name is …. Actually, sorry. I don't want to give my name right now. Is that ok?" The woman at the other end of the phone was friendly, and professional.

"That's absolutely no problem, sir. What can I do for you today?" The nerves got the better of me. I'm not sure exactly what I said, or mumbled, but somehow, I managed to explain that I had the winning numbers for the Mega Millions Lottery. She managed to understand me somehow. I don't know how because I could hardly understand myself.

"Certainly, sir." She said, and then continued. "You will need to bring your ticket into our offices on Abbey Street to be verified, sir. For now, can you call out the verification code on your ticket, please? It's the set of numbers just below the barcode on your ticket. The long set of numbers, sir."

I was still using one hand to hold my other hand steady and not doing a great job at it. In my flustered state, I started to call out the barcode numbers. The phone was still wedged between my head and shoulder, but it was slipping down. I was struggling to keep it in place.

The girl from Lottery corrected me. "No sir, there is a verification number just below the barcode on your ticket. It starts with numbers five, zero, zero." I had a look at the ticket and found what she was looking for. I could feel the phone slipping from my grip and tried to correct its position with my chin. I started reading the numbers out.

"Five, zero, zero, six, nine." Then I shouted, "Shit!" I had lost the battle with the phone, and it fell on the floor. I scrambled to get it back into position. "Are you still there?" I said. "Sorry about that. I dropped the phone." The girl wasn't fazed in fairness to her.

"No problem, sir. Now, can you call out those numbers again, please?" I tried to read the numbers out again, but these numbers are much smaller and there must be about fifty of them. Both of my hands were still shaking.

"I'll need to get my glasses," I lied. I was too nervous and couldn't hold the ticket steady. Then I changed my story. "Actually. I'll bring the ticket into your office tomorrow, to verify it, is that ok?" I wasn't thinking straight. I should have said I'd be in that day. The poor girl must have thought I was a right idiot, but she stayed courteous and professional.

"That's no problem, sir. You can also check that ticket at any of our lottery agents if you wish."

"No, no," I say. "I'll be in tomorrow. Is three o'clock ok? Three o'clock tomorrow." The girl was still professional.

"That's no problem, sir. Are you sure you don't want to give me your name? So we know when you're here."

"No, no, not for now, thanks. I'll see you tomorrow. Thanks for your help."

I went to hang up the phone, but quickly put it back to my ear. Dropping my lottery ticket onto the floor at the same time. "Oh, hello? Are you still there?" I said. She was still there.

"Yes, sir. Was there something else?"

"Do you have a name for me, please? Who will I ask for tomorrow?"

"Could you hold the line please, sir?"

"Sure, no problem, I'll hold." I was put on hold for about a minute, then a male voice came on the line. It was obvious he had already been brought up to speed by the claim's girl.

"Hello, this is Mr Davenport, head of the claims team. I believe congratulations are in order, sir."

Between talking to the automated American voice, the automated Irish voice, the Irish claims team girl, and now Mr Davenport, I'd had enough. My imagination was telling me someone was tracing my call to find out who I was. This fellow had a snooty voice, and I wasn't in the mood to talk or give any more information. I was also trying to see my lottery ticket, which I knew was on the floor, but I couldn't see it.

"Mr Davenport is it?" I said. Then I cut the conversation off. "I have to go. I'll see you tomorrow. I'll be in with my ticket at three o'clock. Thank you." He was about to talk, but I hung up.

I found my ticket under my chair. I was kicking myself. Why did I say tomorrow? Why didn't I say I'll be in today? The ticket still has to be officially verified. Now I have to wait till tomorrow.

I was relieved to get that phone call out of the way, but still wary that the ticket needed to be verified. I felt that I needed to tell someone and get advice, but I knew I couldn't tell anyone, not if I wanted to keep this quiet and stay anonymous. I wanted to phone Claire. Tell her everything will be okay, better than okay. Everything will be great. I dialled her number, but quickly hung up. Let's get this verified first. Just in case.

My head was all over the place. I needed to keep busy, keep the mind occupied. I also wanted to visit my Mother, or my Mother's grave I should say. My sister Catherine and brother Martin are coming home soon. We have plans to celebrate our mother's life. Last April, four weeks after the cancelled wedding. We lost our dear mother to Covid.

Family who had to cancel flights for the wedding in March couldn't fly home for the funeral in April. In fact, even the funeral was more or less cancelled. We had a small service with just a handful of us there because of Covid restrictions.

Mum would talk sense to me if she was still with us. Somehow, that's exactly what seemed to happen. A couple of chance meetings happened from when I set out to visit her grave and getting back home. I realised I could do a lot of good with this. Make a real difference to people's lives. So many people too. I also realised that I would need help. But who? Who could I trust?

Chapter 2

On the way to visit my mother's grave, a woman flagged me down. I wasn't going to stop, but I recognised her. It was Emma. She climbed into my taxi while talking. "Saint Gabriel's nursing home, please." Emma had been one of my mother's carers.

"I thought it was you, Emma. You might not remember me; you were very good to my mother last year." Emma looked up at me. She wasn't wearing her glasses. She squinted her eyes, then recognised me.

"Ah, Billy, how are ye? And God rest your Mother's soul. They were tough times for you all." We had a bit of chitchat. Remembered my mother, which was nice. Emma told me all of the carers loved calling to see my Mother, I already knew that.

"And tell me, how is Benjamin getting on?" I asked. "Did he ever get back home to Nigeria?" There was an uncomfortable silence. Emma got visibly upset all of a sudden.

"I'm sorry Billy, Benjamin passed away in July. He got the Corona Virus and there were complications."

I suddenly felt like I was hit by a ton of bricks. Benjamin was a real character. He was always in a good mood no matter what was thrown his way. All his patients loved him. My Mother always enjoyed it when he called to see her. He'd light up the room with his personality and infectious laugh, which would echo around the house. He was just full of life.

"I'm so sorry, Emma, I didn't know. Didn't he have a family back home?" Emma was getting a tissue from her handbag to dry her eyes.

"Benjamin has three children back in Nigeria. We had a memorial service for him just last week." We arrived at the nursing home. Emma fidgeted for her purse.

"No, don't worry about that, Emma," I said. "I'm not working; this is a lift, a lift for a friend of my mother." Emma thanked me and went off to work. I sat in the car for a while before heading to the cemetery. Thinking of Benjamin and the family he left behind.

I don't like to stay long when I visit a cemetery. It's always cold at a cemetery. Peaceful but cold. As if to say, welcome; thanks for calling by, but don't stay too long, you'll be here long enough, eventually.

I stayed for a while this day. It didn't feel as cold. I was visiting my mother's grave, but I couldn't get Benjamin out of my head. My mother was taken too soon, but she had lived a full life. Benjamin was a young man. I thought a lot about all the good I could do with this money. I could make a difference to so many people's lives.

I wondered what advice my mother would have. She always seemed to do and say the right thing. We didn't have it easy growing up, but that's not to say we had it hard either. We didn't get everything we wanted, but our mother always made sure we had everything we needed.

I remember a particular family on our street had fallen on tough times. Sometimes my mother used to get me to put an envelope in their letter box when they were out. She never told me what was in the envelopes, but young as I was, I had a good idea. The family never called to say thank you. They never knew who was helping them out, or at least they never admitted they knew, I suppose. This annoyed me and on one occasion, I refused to bring the envelope.

I questioned my mother about it. "What is the point if the family doesn't know who gave them help?" I'll never forget what she said to me that day and it was the advice I needed on this day.

"Billy, good deeds should be done with intention; not for attention." I decided to help as many people as I could, but anonymously, like those secret envelopes.

I always kept my circle small and my wall high. I was determined to keep it this way. But I'd need help. Help from outside my circle and beyond my wall. I was going to give as much away to as many people as I could. Anyone and everyone I felt deserved it.

When I left the cemetery, I felt kind of energised. I was a man on a mission. I started a list. People I could help, or even just say thank you to. Benjamin was the first name on my list. Well, his family. Emma was on the list. There were other carers who helped my mother. They were all on my list.

I drove into town and parked the taxi. I decided to treat myself to lunch, but really, I just needed to sit down and sort my head out. I phoned Claire. I needed to talk to her! Maybe we could meet…. have lunch together…. have a chat, talk things through…. if the chat goes well, I could tell her. I just needed to tell someone. I wanted to tell Claire. I had to talk to her at least. Claire didn't answer her phone. I didn't leave a voice message. What would I say?

I've been living and working around this city all my life without noticing things. Well, if I'm honest, I do notice, but choose to ignore them, I suppose. We all do. I noticed a lot yesterday. The poverty around town. Homeless people, lots of them, camped in doorways of derelict buildings with sleeping bags. The lucky ones had a tent to sleep in. They all had carrier bags around them for their miserly possessions.

I could make a difference here with all this money; I can really help people in need. The thing is, no matter how much money I have and try to spread around, I won't be able to do it alone. I could help so many people but I'm not ashamed to say, I don't want to be doing all the work. Why should I? It's about getting the balance right. One thing's for sure, though. I would need help.

It's not just that. I haven't had it too easy myself in life up to now. I'm looking forward to doing whatever the hell I want with this money for myself and my family. Even my family's families. I never wanted a fancy mansion or sports car, but now I can afford it. Who knows? Maybe I will get the house and the car. Maybe when I have that money in the bank, I'll change my mind.

I heard a shout from across the road. "Bill, Bill. Hey Billy. I knew it was you. How the hell are ye?" I looked around. I didn't recognise who it was, so I crossed over the road. It was Kevin Quinn. He was outside O'Connell's pub.

Well, he was at the door holding a pint, half in and half out of the pub. I was in school with Kevin. I've probably only bumped into him a few times since we left school. We're friends, well…. friends on Facebook anyway.

"Look at the head on ye, Billy. How's it going? Are you still driving that poxy taxi?" I wouldn't say Kevin was drunk, but he was under the influence, maybe had a couple of beers on him, and when I say I had only seen him a few times since school, it's true to a point. We all have that friend on Facebook, living the life fantastic. He was either posting photos of himself on an exotic beach somewhere, drinking exotic cocktails, or both. Kevin was that guy, so I'd seen him on Facebook lots of times.

Kevin went to put his arm around me, then remembered social distancing, or the confusion we all have around it now. He stood back. "Come in for a pint, Billy," he said, "My treat, for old times' sake."

"I'm actually driving that poxy taxi today," I told him. "I won't have a drink, but I'll go in for a while. How is life treating you?"

We had lunch; I had lunch, Kevin had lunch, and a couple more beers. He was in great form at first. We talked about school days, the good ol days. Then I got the real story. He was in trouble. Kevin had opened a restaurant just before the lock down last year. He'd borrowed money and poured his savings into it. He poured his heart out to me there and then.

Seems he's had one bad luck experience after another since he left school. He's barely keeping afloat now. He's behind on his loan repayments and his rent. He's tied into a high rent lease for the restaurant near Temple Bar. "What about all those great photos on Facebook?" I enquired.

"A load of shit," was his immediate response. "We all do that, Billy, don't we?" The guy driving 'the poxy taxi' stayed silent and didn't answer this question.

In the middle of all this, Claire phoned me back. She was returning my missed call. I apologised to Kevin and stepped aside for a bit of privacy. The conversation didn't go according to plan.

I answered with, "Hi Claire, thanks for phoning me back. How are you getting on?" She says,

"Not too bad, Billy," and then, before I could talk, she adds, "It's not a great line. I can hardly hear you." It wasn't a great line. The pub wasn't too busy, but there was noise in the background. I carried on talking regardless.

"Claire, I was hoping we could meet, you know…. we need to talk…. this is going on too long." She, no doubt, had our previous phone call fresh in her mind.

"So, you've time to talk now, do you?" I didn't know what she meant.

"Of course, I have time, Claire; I've just had a lot on my mind lately. I'm with a friend now; can I meet up with you somewhere later, for a chat?" Kevin heard me saying the 'with a friend,' bit and shouted over in my direction.

"How are ye, Claire? Don't worry, we're behaving ourselves." There was a brief silence from Claire's end of the phone as she tried to figure things out.

"Well, I've had a lot on my mind too, Billy. What's that noise? I can hardly hear you…… Are you in the pub?" Before I could explain, she shouts. "I'll talk to you when you're not too busy." And she hung up.

I said my goodbyes to Kevin, but not before telling him I knew someone who could help him out. He was grateful, desperate; I suppose. The guy that can help him out is me. Kevin doesn't need to know that.

Are there people out there more in need of help than Kevin? There are so many people more in need of help. Kevin is a friend, a friend in need of help. I'm not trying to save the world; I can help so many people. Kevin might have finally got his lucky break by bumping into me. Who knows, maybe he can help me in return. If I help him bounce back. Maybe he can bounce something back in my direction if I need a favour.

Chapter 3

As I said, I won't be a Billionaire for long. Billy the Billionaire; I don't think so. I'm going to give as much of it away as I can. I'm still writing my list. Kevin has made the cut now. Not sure how I'll help him yet, but I'll definitely do something for him.

I'm thinking about how much I am going to give to my family. Do I need them to know where the money comes from? Do I need them to know it's from me? Could I give large sums away without saying where I got it? There are still a lot of things I need to figure out. Most importantly, I need to verify the ticket before I make any plans.

There was a different twist to the news this evening. A rumour has spread that the winning Billion Euro ticket got lost during a drunken night in town. I think social media has a lot to answer for here. People have been rummaging through the bins in the city centre hoping to find the golden Billion Euro ticket. It's all over the news and social media. I'd laugh only for the fact that I nearly lost the ticket in my own bin.

News sites even had a Hen party from Liverpool on, talking about it. They had been looking for the ticket around town. They were all wearing silly tee shirts with logos on them, such as 'I Won The Billion Euro Jackpot In Dublin' or 'My Husband Won The Billion Euro And All He Got Me Was This Lousy Tee Shirt.' These silly tee shirts have become a bit of a craze in Dublin lately. I met Jane in town a couple of days ago. She was with a few of her friends, and they all had the latest fashion trend, or silly tee shirts. Jane's tee shirt had a caption 'I didn't win the Billion Euro, Because I Got High'

I couldn't help driving past the Lottery offices on my way home, imagining what I'll do when I call in with the ticket tomorrow. Seemed quite enough. I was expecting a few reporters to be hanging around, hoping to get the big scoop. People were just minding their own business or walking in and out of the place with no fuss.

I'm nervous about how I handled the phone call to the Lottery. I don't want to make a fool of myself when I go into their office. I feel calm and decide to phone them again, to make sure they are expecting me as planned.

Same as last time I got my automated American pal, followed by my automated Irish pal. I press number two again. I get talking to someone after a few seconds. Could be the same woman I talked to last time; I'm not too sure. A friendly voice all the same. "Hello National Lottery claims team. How can I help you today?" I'm ready this time.

"Hi, I was talking to one of your colleagues this morning. Mr Davenport was his name. I have an appointment to see him tomorrow. Could you check my lottery ticket verification code, please?" The woman is very calm and professional. Like she gets people calling every day with a Billion Euro ticket to be checked.

"Certainly, sir. Mr Davenport is not available at the moment, but I can check your ticket for you now if you like." I'm more prepared this time and not as nervous.

"Can I call out the verification code for you, please?" The woman is still calm. We both are this time.

"Yes, please call out the verification code; it's the long number underneath the bar code on your ticket." I call out the numbers, all fifty-five of them. I had counted them and even did a practice run to myself beforehand. No embarrassing hiccups this time.

"That sounds good, sir. Congratulations. I am obliged to tell you; we will need to verify your actual ticket here in our office on the National Lottery computer. This will be done by Mr Davenport during your meeting tomorrow." I let out a sigh, a sigh of relief. I was happy with that. It makes sense that the actual ticket needs to be checked.

"I'll be in tomorrow at three o'clock to see Mr Davenport." I tell her.

"Would you like to give me a name, sir? So, I can tell Mr Davenport you called."

"No. Thank you. I don't want to give my name. Thanks for your help." She ended the conversation with.

"Thank you for getting in touch. Best of luck tomorrow."

I feel better about going in after the phone call. Nothing has really changed. The ticket still needs to be officially verified. It doesn't stop my head from spinning, though. I'm wary of making any plans for the money. I can't tell anyone, and I must stay anonymous.

It doesn't stop me from wondering, though. How much money do I need to have no more financial worries? How much do I give to my family? I'm thinking three thousand Euro a week. That's a massive amount of money. You could buy everything you wanted and more.

I calculate it out. Three thousand a week is roughly one hundred and fifty thousand a year. If I had that, every year till retirement age of about sixty-five. That's about five million Euro. That's how I came up with my magic number of five million Euro. A nice round number. A hell of a lot of money for anyone.

I'm thinking at least five million Euro each for my brother and sister. Maybe I could invest a further five million Euro in a retirement fund for them. I need to do this anonymously. I haven't got the money yet. The ticket hasn't been verified and I've already spent twenty million Euro in my head.

I haven't even got to Claire and Jane yet. It will be grand; sure, I'm collecting one thousand million Euro tomorrow. What about Claire, though? We should be celebrating this together. I need to get us back together first. Claire needs to want to get back for the right reasons, though. Not just because of the money. As much as I hope Claire and I sort things out, if she's made her mind up and wants nothing more to do with me, I'll still make sure she's comfortable for the rest of her life.

As for Jane? I worry about the effect this could have on her. I don't want her to give up on her dreams of becoming a vet. I would give her anything and everything she wants. I need to be sensible, though. We'll start her off with a new phone. Any phone she desires, and maybe a bit of pocket money too, I suppose.

Chapter 4

During the Covid lockdown, for some of us, it felt like we were living in an apocalyptic movie of some sort. It was strange times. I feel like I'm in a different movie now. It should be like a Disney movie. All sugar and spice and everything nice. Something doesn't feel right, though. I have an uneasy feeling. Today's the day I collect one Billion Euro. Fasten your seat belts. Button up your overcoats.

I'm King of the World; I'm Dorothy, about to go on the yellow brick road to Oz; I'm Charlie Bucket and I've got the golden ticket to Willy Wonka's Chocolate Factory in my pocket. All well and good. Well and good, except, the thing is, Dorothy and Charlie did not have it all their own way. They both had trouble on their journeys. Maybe I'm on the yellow brick road to the chocolate factory or maybe I'm on a Titanic journey.

I felt surprisingly calm. I was ready, or I thought I was ready. Are you ever ready to collect one Billion Euro? I've decided to go into town and plan my journey for later. I look out and, as I do habitually, make sure the coast is clear. No such luck, the coast wasn't clear. Mrs Fogarty is at her gate across the road. She has a posse of her bingo buddies with her. They're talking, whispering. Pretty sure they're talking about me. I can almost hear her say, 'Search every gas station, residence, warehouse, farmhouse, hen house, outhouse, doghouse and Billy's house.'

I make a dash for my car. I've been spotted, though; they stop talking and all look over at me in tandem. "Good morning, ladies, lovely weather we're getting," I say to them as I'm fidgeting to get my car door open. Mrs Fogarty then says.

"Hello Billy, are you off to collect the Billion Euro jackpot, then?" At least that's what I imagined she said. Got to get a grip on myself.

"Yes, Mrs Fogarty. I'm off to work. Have a nice day, ladies."

The news comes on my radio when I start the car. It's the same old news, still talking about the lottery. I go to switch the radio off when suddenly we got. 'A spokesperson from The National Lottery has said that the Billion Euro jackpot winner has been in contact. They have made arrangements to call and collect the jackpot. We've offered our full support.'

I nearly crashed into my bin again. What did they mean by, 'The Jackpot Winner has been in contact?' I was a bit shaken. I never gave my name. 'Okay, stay calm.' I tell myself. They never said they knew who it was. Just that the winner had been in contact. In fairness, I had been in contact. It just spooked me hearing about it on the news.

This unsettled me. It felt more real now, what I was about to do. I wasn't prepared for the day ahead, never mind beyond that. I felt like a fugitive now. Everyone wants to know who the Billion Euro jackpot winner is. I reverse out of my driveway, carefully avoiding my bin.

The bingo buddies stand silently while staring at my every movement. I remind myself that nobody knows about this. I also remind myself to stay calm and collected, if I want it to stay that way.

I drive into town and find a parking spot near the Lottery head office. There is a bus stop close to the Lottery offices. I've decided to get the bus in later. If I get a taxi, I'll probably know the driver and there might be too many uncomfortable questions. With the bus, I can simply walk off at the stop and straight in the front door. It doesn't look like there are any reporters or photographers around.

People are walking up and down the street with the occasional person walking in or out of the Lottery offices. Anyone, including me, could just walk in or out of those doors with little attention. Next time I'm here, I'll be collecting one Billion Euro.

I'm wondering what sort of plans the Lottery staff are making for today. Maybe I could just walk in now, get it over with. I'm at a bit of a loose end now. I'm just waiting until three o'clock. I'll stick to my plan, though.

Can I really walk out of there today with one Billion Euro and not tell anyone? Can I really do this alone? The media storm around this has been crazy. Everyone wants to know who won the Billion Euro. It's been constantly on the news like there was nothing else to talk about.

I decided to wander around and get some fresh air. I'll phone Claire later, see if she'll talk to me. I'm wishing things were better between us. Wish I could tell her or even bring her with me today. I can't tell her today, though. Not the way things are between us.

There's a big guy with sunglasses and a black leather jacket walking up and down Henry Street. He's a bit shifty looking, and he's watching everything. He's definitely not a reporter, but he's obviously looking for someone. He reminds me of Arnold Schwarzenegger in the Terminator movie, but the truth is, he looks like many a dodgy character you'd see floating around Dublin city. I imagine he's looking for me but remind myself again to stay calm. What's happening today is all good. Great things are about to happen.

I'm thinking that I could stand in the middle of town handing out fifty euro notes all day, or all week, and it wouldn't even put a dent in one Billion Euro. I could, but not anonymously. I'm still adding names to my list. Names of people I am going to help and good causes I can help. It's a long list now, but not long enough yet.

I find a café and order breakfast. I can see the world go by outside from my window seat. There is still a bit of social distancing going on outside. A few people are still wearing protective face masks. A group of teenagers walk by, all of them wearing silly tee shirts like Jane's. I wonder if there will be new tee shirts out tomorrow. By then it will have been announced that the Mega Millions Jackpot has been claimed. Anonymously, of course. I've got to keep my name and face off those silly tee shirts.

There is a dog wandering around outside. I've seen the dog before, It's Bruce's dog. Bruce, and his dog, The Duke, are part of the homeless community. They would be well-known characters in Dublin city. It's unusual to see the dog on its own, as the two of them are usually inseparable. I'll just keep an eye out for him.

I see a man acting suspiciously in a clothes shop across the road. I don't know him, but I've seen him around town. He's a dodgy character who sells dodgy merchandise. He's not the type of guy you would want to bump into. The man looks like he's hiding from someone. He's standing in the shop doorway, and he keeps looking up and down the street anxiously. Maybe that Terminator guy is looking for him and not me, after all.

The man clumsily tries to take an overcoat off a shop mannequin displayed inside the shop window. It's one of those long beige Mackintosh overcoats that Humphrey Bogart was famous for wearing. This guy is no Humphrey Bogart. He's more of a Humpty Dumpty because he's after falling inside the window while grappling with the mannequin. It now looks like he's fighting with the mannequin as he struggles to take the overcoat off it.

There are two elderly women standing outside the shop. They are laughing hysterically as they watch the show. I try to stifle my own laughter from my window seat across the road. Winning the fight, he puts on the overcoat and hurries out of the shop, holding the collar up to cover as much of his face as he can. He walks as fast as he can down Henry Street, then disappears around a corner. The owner of the clothes shop rushes out, looks back at the now mangled mannequin in his window display. He obviously thinks better than trying to retrieve the Mackintosh overcoat.

I decide to have a walk around town. Maybe make sure that dog is all right. I notice that for all the hustle and bustle in town, there are still a lot of businesses closed. Shops with shutters down. Homeless people sleeping in the doorways.

I'm still looking for that dog. Not paying much attention, when suddenly I get knocked off my feet. Knocked flat on my back. The guy with the Mackintosh overcoat has come charging back around the corner and runs straight into me.

"Get out of my fucken way ye stupid bollix" He shouts at me. Before I can get back on my feet again, he's already gone. Running down the street with that Terminator guy chasing after him. The two elderly women are across the road and laughing hysterically again. I'm a bit shook but not hurt after this encounter. People carry on with their own business as I straighten myself up. Nobody knows who I am, or cares. I'm anonymous in this town. I intend to keep it that way.

I see that dog again. He's back with his owner in one of those empty doorways. The Terminator guy passes me too, and he's in a foul mood. Looks like the guy with the overcoat has got away from him this time.

I'm now thinking maybe I should phone Claire; we could meet, we could talk and, hopefully, sort everything out. There's still plenty of time before I go into the Lottery today. I could tell her we won. Tell her we have no more worries. She could even come in with me to collect the winnings.

It would be great if I had her with me today. I need her with me. So, I phone her. Claire seemed happy to hear from me. In fact, when she answered the phone, she seemed not only happy but also relieved that I phoned. "Hi Claire, how are you getting on?" Cheerfully, she replied.

"Oh Billy, good to hear from you. I was just thinking of you. I was just about to phone you, in fact." I was encouraged by her response.

"Great Claire, I'm actually in town. I was hoping we could meet, maybe go for a coffee and a chat?" I could hear a muffled voice in the background, as if someone else was talking to her.

"Billy, I can't really talk right now." She whispered the next line. "Mrs Fogarty has just sat down beside me and she's all ears." I thought it was strange that Mrs Fogarty was with her,

"Where are you Claire? Maybe I could come over to you. I'd love to meet you. We need to talk." She was still whispering,

"Billy, I'm kind of busy right now. Can I call you back in about an hour, when I can talk properly?" I could feel the frustration from Claire in her awkward situation. I was also wondering how Mrs Fogarty could be sitting beside her, so I asked what I felt was a reasonable question.

"Claire, are you on the bus?" Her response was raised now,

"On the bus! What makes you think I'm on the bus, Billy?" She then went back to whispering. "I have…. I have an appointment, Billy. I could meet you later. I can't really talk with…. with, you know who. I could meet you at three o'clock, Billy."

Now it was awkward for me. I could hardly meet Claire at three o'clock, then have the two of us saunter into the Lottery office to collect one Billion Euro. I would have to meet her and explain things.

"Claire, I'm kind of busy at three o'clock. I sort of have an appointment too. Are you sure we can't meet earlier?" Her response was whispered, but she might as well have been shouting.

"Billy, I have to go. Phone me back when you actually have time to meet me. Or do I have to book an appointment with you too? Bye." End of conversation. She hung up the phone.

I was getting disheartened by the Claire situation now. What more could I do? It was Claire who moved out, after all. I'm sure she's not telling me something. I can't figure it out, can't figure her out. I need to focus on the day ahead now. Claire will come round when she is ready. At least I hope she will. With all my focus on staying anonymous today, I'm also realising there's a fine line between being anonymous and being alone.

It's getting closer to the time now. I drive home. I have my plan and I'll stick to it. I get my lottery ticket out from its hiding place in the shed. I'm still nervous about handling it or carrying it around. I put it in my pocket. For extra safety, I secure my pocket closed with a couple of safety pins, so it can't slip out. Can't be too careful.

I check the bus timetable, again. I had already checked several times. There is a bus due at two twenty-five. Perfect, that will get me in with time to spare. It's a twenty-minute journey. Better to be there early and suss things out.

With my plan, the bus will stop near the Lottery head office. I'll make sure I'm the last person off the bus at that stop. Get off the bus, keep the head down, then walk straight into the Lottery office and ask for Mr Davenport. A simple plan. I just get the money and get out of there as quickly as I can with as little fuss as possible.

I'm still nervous about this getting out. I'm determined to stay anonymous. If I stick to my plan everything should be ok. Time to go. The bus is due in ten minutes and it's a five-minute walk from my house to the bus stop. Surprisingly, the coast is clear when I leave the house, a good start.

I'm at the bus stop in good time, but I start to question myself now. Why am I on my own? I'm going to collect one Billion Euro, the biggest lottery prize ever, and here I am, alone at a bus stop. Nobody knows who I am or what I'm about to do. Do I even know what I'm about to do? What about Clair? She should be with me.

The bus arrives on time. I sit downstairs at the back so I can see what's going on ahead of me. No major incidents as the bus travels towards the city centre. All good so far. I'm told the journey will take approximately nineteen minutes on the Dublin Bus App. The App is spot on. I arrive at my bus stop at two forty-four. My plan is going like clockwork.

I remind myself again, stick to the plan, Billy, the simple plan. I'm at the back of the bus, downstairs. A few people move towards the door to get off at my bus stop, about six people. I let them go ahead of me. All going according to plan so far.

I follow behind. All good so far. I'm ready to go into the Lottery head office and collect one Billion Euro. My attention is suddenly drawn across the road, though. A man with sunglasses and a black leather jacket is standing there. He's staring over in my direction. It's the same guy I saw this morning, Terminator guy! What is he doing here?

Chapter 5

Nothing could have prepared me for what happened next. It all happened so fast, too. The man across the road had caught my eye and unsettled me. It's that Terminator guy I saw in town earlier. I step off the bus. I'm watching the Terminator guy and not paying attention to what's going on ahead of me.

At the entrance to the Lottery office, there is a bit of a commotion going on. A few people have gathered around someone near the door. I wasn't sure at first, but then I realised it's the guy who bumped into me, crashed into me, this morning. He's still wearing the Mackintosh overcoat.

I can't think straight. I tell myself: 'just stick to the plan.' I'm already walking towards the door of the Lottery office.

It's three or four meters to the door. I'm thinking of changing my plan now, but there's too much going on. If I change course, I'll just end up in the middle of them all and I don't want to bump into that man again. I keep my head down as I get to the front door.

Its large glass double doors. I push the door open, and I walk inside.

The reception area is a spacious, pristine area. Not huge, but bigger than I expected. There is a receptionist seated at a desk to my right. She's busy on the phone but is distracted by what's going on outside. It's a glass fronted building so you can see all the goings on out there. Two people come down a set of stairs to the left. Lottery staff, by the looks of them. They want to see what's going on outside. Nobody pays me any attention. Like I'm invisible, or anonymous, I suppose.

One of the new guys on the scene catches the receptionist's attention with a waving arm and whispers to her as loud as he can, "Is that him?" The receptionist is still busy on the phone and looking outside at the same time. She shrugs her shoulders, as if to say, she doesn't know. For a second, I thought they were talking about me, but no, they were all fascinated with what's going on outside.

I'm thinking maybe I should just get out of there. Leave and come back another time. More people have stopped outside to see what the commotion is all about. More people come down the stairs to the reception area, too. They all ignore me and look to see what's going on outside. I'm in the middle of them, so I decide to edge away over to the reception desk.

The guy from this morning with the Mackintosh overcoat is waving his arms around shouting "Jackpot, Jackpot, it's me. I'm Jackpot!" He has what looks like a lottery ticket in one of his hands. My first instinct is to put my hand in my pocket to make sure I still have my lottery ticket. It's still there, secured with the safety pins. I'm wondering could he have switched it this morning when he knocked me over. No, I didn't have my ticket with me then. Could he have followed me home and switched tickets? Realistically, no.

Even though I must have checked the ticket one hundred times, I'm regretting not checking it again before I left the house now. I'm wondering, could there even be two winning tickets for the jackpot? No, I remind myself. It's been nonstop on the news. There is only one winning ticket. I have that ticket in my pocket. Secured with two safety pins.

Things are getting a bit crazy outside now. Getting a bit crazy inside the reception area, too. More people have arrived downstairs to see what's going on and the girl from reception is over near the door now looking out the windows. I stand meekly at the reception desk. Not knowing what to do or where to look.

And there is Sandra now. Maybe I should have mentioned it earlier, but my daughter Jane's mother is well known journalist Sandra Birch. Sandra is an old flame of mine. Things didn't work out between us, but we were blessed with the wonderful Jane. I always felt that Sandra thought I came from the wrong side of the tracks, the wrong side of the River Liffey even. Sandra is married to media photographer Michael. They have a family of their own and a lovely house on the right side of the river. They both work for the newspaper and media group Dublin Today.

Dublin Today has an office not too far from here and Sandra's never too far from the big stories. It was only a matter of time before she showed up, really, with all the fuss outside. I hadn't factored Sandra into this because there was no need with my simple plan. I need to get out of here before she sees me, but I'm kind of stuck now. No way out of here without being noticed. Stuck in here and no one has noticed me yet.

All eyes, including mine, are on the man outside. Someone from the reception area has recognised him. "That's Jack Potter," he says loudly. "They call him Jackpot." He then pauses before exclaiming. "Holy shit! Has Jackpot won the Billion Euro Jackpot?"

Jack Potter, as I know him now, is lapping up all the attention he's getting outside. He's in better form than the man who knocked me over this morning. I'm trying to stay out of sight from the people outside. I can't let Sandra see me here. The Terminator guy is still across the road and he's looking even shiftier than he did this morning.

There are face masks at the side of the reception desk. Lottery merchandise. I take one and put it on. The mask helps cover my face. It has a lottery logo on the front. Two big letters M. The MM stands for Mega Millions.

I can't hear all that's going on outside, but I can see it. People have stopped on the street to see what is happening. Even cars have stopped on the road.

Sandra has manoeuvred herself to the front and is now close to Jack Potter. Sandra has a reputation for getting her story, the whole dirty story. Sandra Birch, or 'Nosey Bitch,' as they call her in certain circles in the city, and believe me, she gets called much worse than that.

There must be about fifty people gathered outside now, and I'm sort of stuck inside. I don't know what to do or where I can go. Sandra is the only person who would know me out there. Well, Sandra and Michael, that is. I can't see Michael, but if Sandra is here, Michael is sure to be here, too. He's probably in the background somewhere, taking photographs. Sandra and Michael leave nothing to chance.

That's how they get the best stories. I've no chance of escaping from here unnoticed.

The girl from reception has finally seen me and comes back in behind her desk. "Sorry Sir, I didn't notice you with all the excitement out there. Now, how can I help you?" She's talking to me but looking over my shoulder at the circus going on outside. I can tell she's keen to deal with me quickly so she can get back to see all the action.

"I'm here to see Mr Davenport; I've an appointment for three o'clock." I tell her. I have her full attention now. She's a bit taken aback, flustered, but she switches to professional mode at the same time.

"Oh, certainly, sir. Can I have your name please?" I'm nervous but focused.

"Mr Davenport is expecting me. I don't want to give my name for now," I tell her.

The receptionist picks up her phone, but then realises the man I have an appointment with, Mr Davenport, has just arrived down the stairs to the reception area.

"What's going on?" he snorts. "Get back to your desks." The receptionist tries to get his attention, but he's over at the window now, looking out while directing the rest of his staff to move on.

"Mr Davenport, that's him. He's gone public after all." One of the Lottery staff has his attention now. Mr Davenport ponders for a few seconds while trying to figure out what is happening. Then he starts barking orders.

"John, try to get him in here before he speaks to the reporters, and don't let anyone else in those doors. Mathew, where is Mathew?" He realises Mathew is standing right beside him. "Mathew, get Oliver down here now." He looks around again. "Where's McGrath? Why isn't McGrath here minding the door?"

Too late regarding the reporters. Sandra has her microphone out and is addressing Jack Potter outside. "Jack, is that the Billion Euro ticket you have there?" Jack is still waving his arms about. He has a lottery ticket in one of his hands.

"Jackpot!" He shouts. "I 've won it. It's me and she's not getting a fucking penny either. None of them are!" He's talking to Sandra, well, more like shouting at her. But he's looking across the road. He's making sure the Terminator guy can hear every word.

Some of the crowd start cheering and clapping hands at this point. Cars that have stopped to see the commotion beep their horns. Sandra continues talking to Jack.

"Congratulations Jack Potter. You're now one of the richest men in Ireland. Who's not getting a penny, Jack?"

Jack Potter looks at Sandra. He looks a bit deflated all of a sudden and has stopped waving his arms and shouting. He looks Sandra in the eye and says,

"Tell them all to go fuck themselves. They won't get another penny out of me. Put that in your rag of a newspaper for them to see." The door to the Lottery offices suddenly opens. It's John, and a burly security guard. McGrath, I presume. They're following Mr Davenport's orders and trying to get Jack Potter inside.

"Sir, sir. Come inside, please." Jack turns to the open door and walks inside; McGrath doesn't let anyone else in. The crowd is still cheering and clapping outside. Jack just stands there with his hands on his hips, looking around the reception area. He looks at McGrath, the security guard, and says,

"I told you; Jack Potter doesn't do fucking appointments." McGrath looks away sheepishly and locks the door to stop anyone else from getting inside. The locked door stops people from getting out, too.

The receptionist tries to get Mr Davenport's attention. Half- heartedly now because all eyes are on Jack Potter. Mr Davenport steps towards Jack and offers his hand to him. Jack takes a step back away from Mr Davenport, while looking at him suspiciously. Jack is looking all around the room of strangers he's found himself in.

51

A bit put out by the snub, Mr Davenport addresses Jack. "Nice to meet you, sir. I'm Edward Davenport. You've caught us off guard somewhat, sir. You said you were not going public." He then barks at the security guard, "McGrath, dim those blinds, give us some privacy." McGrath turns the blinds. We can see the circus outside now, but they can't see inside, which is a relief for me.

I'm still wondering if there is any way I can get out of there. Sandra and Michael are both at the windows now. Trying to see in between the blinds. It's getting even crazier out there. Word must have spread around town that the Jackpot winner is claiming the Billion Euro. The Gardai have arrived because of the crowd and resulting traffic jams. The sight of the Gardai seems to have sent the Terminator guy on his way.

There are a handful of us now in the reception area. We have Jack Potter, who's erratic and nobody is sure how to deal with him, Mr Davenport, who is all business-like but nervous of Jack's behaviour, McGrath on security at the door, making sure nobody else gets in, a couple more lottery staff waiting for instructions, and the receptionist, at her desk, looking busy on the phone. Then there's me. I'm just standing near the reception desk, like a spare part. I feel like an extra in a movie scene.

With all the chaos going on, I'm realising even more so the importance of staying anonymous. That is, if I have even won the Billion Euro. I'm still wearing the face mask and there is no way I am taking it off now. I'm watching Jack Potter. Something's not right. I can sense it; Jack has gone quiet now, too quiet. He's not saying a word. Mr Davenport is talking to him and it's as if Jack thinks he's in a police station and is under arrest. Like he won't talk and has a right to remain silent.

"Is that your lottery ticket, Mr Potter?" Mr Davenport is talking to Jack, who has a tight grip on his lottery ticket. It doesn't look like he wants to hand it over. Jack then bursts out laughing suddenly, a strange laugh, which makes everyone in the reception area uncomfortable. He still has a vice-like grip on his ticket. He's laughing to himself.

The phone at reception is hopping throughout this and keeping the receptionist busy. No doubt it's reporters trying to get through to get the big scoop. I'm still standing at the reception desk. The only person who's noticed me is the receptionist, and she's busy on the phone. I gently remind her I have an appointment to see Mr Davenport.

Mr Davenport, hearing his name mentioned, glances over at me. I catch his eye. "Hi, I phoned yesterday. We have a meeting at three o'clock today," I say to him. Mr Davenport looks at me, then back to Jack, but says nothing.

He looks confused. I then say, "Is there anywhere we can speak in private, Mr Davenport?" Mr Davenport is getting no sense from Jack, who is still laughing and mumbling under his breath. He walks over to me with his hand outstretched to greet me.

"And you are?" He says tentatively. I shake his outstretched hand.

"If you don't mind, I don't want to give my name for now. Is that ok?" He's still confused and just nods his head in agreement while looking at me, then looking at Jack. I repeat my question. "Is there anywhere we can talk in private, Mr Davenport?" He looks straight at me now.

"Certainly, sir. Come this way, and please; call me Edward." He barks at one of his colleagues beside him. "We'll take suite three, as planned." He then leads me towards a lift. He takes a set of keys out of his pocket. He opens the lift door with one of his keys and gestures for me to go inside.

I feel like Charlie Bucket getting in the lift at the chocolate factory with Willie Wonka. Then he suddenly gestures for Jack to get in the lift. I wasn't expecting this. Has Mr Davenport got his wires crossed? Does he think me, and Jack Potter are together? Jack is still mumbling but joins us in the lift. We go up one floor before the lift door opens. Not a word was spoken in the lift. I'm feeling uncomfortable. We all are. Jack is just smiling and nodding at the two of us.

Mr Davenport leads us out of the lift. He's all business-like now. "Follow me please, gentlemen," he says, while leading us down a corridor to an office door. He opens the door with one of his keys. Jack and I follow him into the office. I'm a bit bemused. As we're walking into the office, I say,

"Mr Davenport, do you mind if we talk in private?" He turns and looks at me, then at Jack. He totally misreads the situation again.

"Certainly, gentlemen," he says. Then addresses Jack Potter. "I will need that lottery ticket you have there." Jack quickly puts the ticket in his pocket. Mr Davenport looks at me, but I don't know what to say, so I say nothing. "I'll give you both a few minutes." he says to me, then addresses Jack Potter again. "I'll need that lottery ticket, sir. To authenticate it, you understand." He then turns and walks out. Leaving me and Jack on our own. I suppose to talk in private.

Now it's just me and Jack. Mr Davenport seems to think that I'm with Jack Potter, and Jack probably thinks I work for the Lottery. Jack takes his lottery ticket back out of his pocket. He's clutching it tightly. It looks torn and ragged. He looks at me; he doesn't remember me from this morning. How would he? Besides, I'm still wearing the face mask. I decide to try and suss him out and say to him, "So, what are you going to spend all that money on, Jack?" He looks at me. He's smiling. Then he suddenly blurts out.

"Got ye. I got ye, mister." I was half expecting a film crew to burst in. Have I been pranked like in one of those stupid television shows? Nothing happens. Jack hands me his lottery ticket. Or what's left of it. I take it from him reluctantly. If he thinks he's won the Billion Euro, he's in trouble. It's torn and mulchy from his sweaty hands.

His mood has changed again now. He's got a serious look on his face. "Listen, mister," he says, looking me straight in the eye. "This has gotten way out of hand. I never said I won. I just said my name is Jackpot. That's what they call me. I'm Jackpot! I was in the wrong fucking place at the wrong fucking time, that's all. I was ducking out of Damo's way. Him and his fucking brother have been chasing after me all week. "

He pauses for breath. He's sweating now and flustered. He continues with his rant. "That dumb security guard downstairs wouldn't let me inside. Said I needed a fucking appointment or something. I told the dumb fucker I was Jackpot, and Jackpot doesn't do fucking appointments. He still wouldn't let me in. That fucker Damo was across the road, and I knew the chicken-shit wouldn't come over while the security guard was there."

Jack is looking hot and bothered now. He takes his overcoat off. He looks around the room, looking for somewhere to hang the overcoat. Then he hands it to me while still talking. "What does the dumb security guard do, then? The dumb ass disappears inside. People then started pointing at me then, saying I had won the jackpot. Fucking idiots. But Damo stayed away from me. The chicken shit."

He points to the torn ragged lottery ticket which I'm holding on the palm of my hand. "See that ticket, pal? There's a fucking bin outside full of them. I just picked one up and started waving it around. It got me a fucking appointment, though. Didn't it?" He has a little laugh to himself and mutters under his breath, "The dumb ass fuckers."

I was just standing there; I didn't know what to say. Then Jack sets off again. "You see that coat?" He points to his overcoat, which I'm holding for him. "That's all I have to my fucking name now, that and the clothes I'm wearing. I got divorced this week, and the bitch took everything, her and her two useless brothers. She took the lot. And they're still chasing me for more."

I'm shocked and trying to get my head around what's happening. All my plans. All my 'stick to the plan, Billy.' But here I am. In the Lottery head office with Jack Potter. The man who knocked me flat on my back this morning and called me 'a stupid bollix.' Not even that. I'm holding his overcoat for him, too.

Jack is looking restless. He continues ranting, but also laughing at the same time. "I bet that nosey bitch of a reporter is spreading the word now. They'll all think I won the lottery and none of them are getting a fucking penny." He walks over to the window and looks outside. There is a crowd out there which seems to be growing by the minute. They are waiting with anticipation. Waiting for the Billion Euro winner to come outside.

"Look at all those fucking assholes out there," he says. "I fucking showed them." He turns to me then and sees his overcoat. "Give me that fucking coat; they might as well have everything." He grabs the overcoat off me and goes to open the window, as if to throw the overcoat out. He's struggling at the window when there's a knock on the door. It's Mr Davenport. He opens the door a little and sticks his head around to see inside.

"How are you getting on, gentlemen?" He says. He's looking around the room nervously. Trying to figure out what's going on. I go over to Jack Potter near the window. I take the overcoat back off him. I can't resist looking outside. The crowd outside has got bigger. They're waiting for the Billion Euro winner to come out. Waiting for Jack Potter. But it's me; I'm the one they're really waiting for.

I begin to wonder to myself. Maybe I can give them what they want. Like I said, 'I don't want to be a Billionaire.' The crowd outside has given me a glimpse of what might happen if people find out who really won the Billion Euro. Maybe there's a way of giving the people their Billionaire winner and for me to stay anonymous too. I'd need Jack Potter on board. If I can get Jack on board, everyone will get what they want.

Mr Davenport is still waiting at the door. He looks worried now. He looks at me, then Jack, then back at me again. I say to him, "Mr Davenport, Edward, we're nearly ready. Can you give us a few more minutes, please?" This seems to put him at ease a little.

"Certainly, gentlemen," he says. He goes to close the door. I call him back.

"Oh, Edward, one more thing." I quickly open the safety pins holding my lottery ticket secure. I take the ticket out of my pocket and hold it out towards Edward. "Could you check this, please? You said you need to authenticate it."

Edward walks briskly into the room now. His eyes are fixed on the lottery ticket in my hand. I now realise he has been waiting for this moment since they announced they sold the winning ticket in Ireland. This is his moment, too. Edward thinks the winner is going public now. He's spruced himself up a bit. He has got himself ready to face the media with the Billion Euro winner by his side. The photos, the interviews. He's ready.

Edward gently takes the lottery ticket out of my hand as if he's handling a new-born baby, or a bomb, even. Maybe the ticket is a bomb and things are about to explode. Edward looks past me, he looks at Jack, and says, "Mr Potter, you are entitled to accompany me while I authenticate your ticket. Would you like to follow me, gentlemen, please?"

Jack is just staring at the lottery ticket in Edward's hand. He's fascinated by the way Edward is holding it. So gently and tenderly. Jack walks towards Edward at the door. I'm still holding Jack's overcoat. I have it draped over my arm. I hold this arm out and stop Jack in his tracks.

"Wait, Jack," I say to him. "Edward said he'd give us a few more minutes in private." I look at Edward. I can see that he's already checked the numbers. He has a wry smile. He knows this is the ticket. He still needs to authenticate it on the lottery system, though. I say to him, "Edward, you go on ahead there and check that, me and Jack here need to have a private chat."

"Certainly, sir," he says. He's looking at me. He's a bit taken aback. "We didn't get your name yet, sir."

"I didn't give my name, Mr Davenport. I'm keeping that to myself for now, if you don't mind." He turns to one of his colleagues in the hall behind him, "Oliver, they have handed me this ticket to authenticate. You're a witness to this, Oliver." He then turns back to me and Jack in the room. "This won't take long, gentlemen. Oliver here will be available if you need anything in the meantime." He closes the door.

It's me and Jack alone in the room again. Jack is looking at me. He saw me handing over the ticket. Not his ticket, my ticket. I can see him trying to work things out in his head. He's figured out that I'm not lottery staff. He's figured out what has happened. Jack looks at me suspiciously.

"I never got your name either, pal. Who the fuck are you?"

I walk past Jack to the window and look outside. There's a huge crowd out there. Looks like more reporters have arrived. The Gardai are trying to keep the traffic moving on the road. I gesture for Jack to come over and look outside. He shuffles over beside me at the window.

"Jack, they're all out there waiting for you. Waiting for you to walk out of here with the Billion Euro Jackpot." Jack looks out. He doesn't look fazed by the crowd out there. He thinks for a couple of seconds, then says.

"Stupid fucking idiots." Then he looks at me suspiciously. "I think they're waiting for you, pal. It's you they're waiting for. Isn't it?"

We're disturbed by a knock on the door. I go over and open it. I only open the door halfway and look out. Mr Davenport is standing there. Oliver is just over his shoulder and there are a few more lottery staff standing behind him. I can tell by their expressions that the ticket has been authenticated, and the news is good. Mr Davenport is bending his neck to look past me and the door to see Jack Potter.

"All good Mr Davenport?" I say to him. He tries to be as professional as possible but can't contain his excitement. He motions to enter the room, but I don't budge from the doorway. I still have the door only half open and don't let him pass. He stops where he is, still bending his neck to see inside the room.

Then he looks at me and says, "Congratulations, we've authenticated the ticket." He has the lottery ticket in his hand. He's holding it gingerly. He holds it up for me to see. Then says proudly, "This is the winning ticket of The Mega Millions Jackpot of one Billion Euro." The lottery staff in the corridor behind him all start clapping hands and cheering congratulations.

I knew it was the winning ticket. I still needed it confirmed, though. I've had a rollercoaster day. The last half an hour in particular. I suddenly feel emotional. Claire should be here, and Jane. They should both be here with me.

Here I am just after being confirmed as the winner of one Billion Euro and I have a pompous snob standing in front of me and a reckless thug in the room behind me. I gather my thoughts quickly and just say,

"Thank you, Mr Davenport." I gently go to close the door as Mr Davenport says,

"Please, call me Edward." I quickly open the door again.

"Is that my ticket you have there, Edward?"

"Yes, Mr…" He pauses, realising he doesn't know my name.

"Thank you, Edward." I take the ticket out of his hand. You would think I had ripped his hand off. He nearly falls over while following the flight of the ticket as I take it, and he bumps his head off the half-open door with an almighty thud. He looked a bit faint for a few seconds. Oliver steps in and helps steady him on his feet. The look on his face was nearly worth the Billion Euro.

"Edward!" I say to him, "we need five more minutes, please." As I go to close the door, I notice more lottery staff further down the corridor behind Edward. They have one of those giant cheques. The ones you see in the newspapers or on television when someone goes public winning the lottery. I close the door.

With the door closed, I lean back against it. I have my lottery ticket in my hand. For a few seconds, I had forgotten Jack was in the room. I say to myself, but out loud. "Fuck this shit!" I quickly come to my senses again and see Jack Potter. He's standing with his hands on his hips and just staring at me. He is still standing near the window and repeats what I said, but more vigorously.

"Fuck this shit is right pal!" He starts walking around the room erratically. "Fuck this shit! What the fuck is going on? And who the hell are you, anyway?

I realise I'm still holding Jack's overcoat over my arm. I can still see him taking it from the shop this morning. I think of him crashing into me afterwards and calling me a 'stupid bollix.' Who'd have thought I'd find myself alone in a room with him now? Not even that. I'm about to make him an offer he couldn't have dreamed of. Nobody could.

I hand Jack back his overcoat. I'm thinking if this overcoat really is all that he has to his name, he couldn't possibly say no to my offer. "Mr Potter." I catch his attention. "Mr Potter, I have a plan, and you can be a part of it. Maybe you were in the right place at the right time after all today."

Jack is looking out the window now. He looks anxious, like he did this morning when he was in the clothes shop. He's probably wondering what's going on and why he's still

in the room, why McGrath, the security guard, hasn't been
sent up to kick him out.

"Mr Potter, I need a favour from you. A big favour, and
I'll make it worth your while. Are you interested?" His ears
perk up. He's realising there might be something in this for
him.

"What sort of favour are we talking about, pal?" Before
I get a chance to answer him, he says, "You're gonna need
security and things. I know people. I can get you anything
you need, pal, anything." I look out the window again. Still
mayhem out there.

"Jack…. Do you mind if I call you Jack?" He looks at me
menacingly.

"My friends call me Jackpot, but you can call me Jack for
now. What's this favour you need, pal? Can I call you Pal?
Or are you going to tell me who the fuck you really are?…
And why the hell don't you take that fucking mask off?" I
take a deep breath.

"Jack, have a look at that crowd outside the window.
They want to see the Billion Euro jackpot winner. They're
out there waiting for you because they think you won it. But
you're right Jack, I have the winning ticket here." I show Jack
the ticket. He's looking out the window but glances over.
"Jack, there's nothing to stop me handing this ticket to that
Davenport fella, collecting my money, and walking off out

of here into the sunset. I don't know you and I owe you nothing. But I can tell you're in trouble, you told me so yourself. Maybe I can help you."

I point to his overcoat, which he has scruffily rolled up under his arm. "You said that all you have is right there under your arm. What if I could change that, Jack? A favour for a favour and I'll make it worth your while." He walks away from the window, closer to me.

He's a bit too close for comfort. He has an intimidating presence. I back away and move towards the window. "You're right, Jack. The Billion Euro winner will need security. Everyone will want a piece of them. There will be no hiding…" Jack interrupts me mid-sentence.

"If Jack can't get it, it can't be got, pal. I know people. It'll cost ye though, but fuck it, you can afford it. You're gonna need…" I stop him mid-sentence.

"Wait, wait, you're missing the point, Jack. Nobody knows who I am, and I want to keep it that way. If nobody knows who I am, then I won't need security. What if you were to walk out of here and tell them what they already believe? Tell them you won the Billion Euro. That way, the public has their man. I can stay anonymous, and I make it worth your while. Everyone wins Jack. What do you think?"

He has a puzzled look on his face while he contemplates what I just said. Suddenly, he bursts out with, "Fuck this shit.

I'll be in all the papers and on the television, too. Everyone will know who Jackpot is." He's not complaining, though. His eyes have lit up. He's imagining himself as being 'the top man,' about town. "Just wait till the lads see me, then they'll know. I'll fucking show them." He walks over to the window and goes to open it.

"Hold it, Jack." I say to him, "what are you doing, Jack?" Too late, he has the window open, and he's shouting out to the crowd below.

"I'm Jackpot! The name's Jackpot. Write that down." The people outside start cheering up at Jack in appreciation. I stay away from the window. The commotion has caused Edward and Oliver to come into the room. Edward sees Jack at the window, but there's no way he's going to intervene. He barks at Oliver.

"Close that window, Oliver!" Oliver nervously approaches the window. He manages to get it closed without upsetting or unsettling Jack, who is back in the middle of the room now. He's rubbing his hands together with excitement and talking to himself, but out loud.

"Wait till that bitch and her brothers see me. This will teach them not to mess with Jack Potter." Edward looks at me, as if looking for me to say something. He's careful to avoid getting in Jack's way. It's clear by their expressions that Edward and Oliver don't know what to make of things.

Jack goes back to the now closed window. He attempts to hand his overcoat to Edward but Edward gestures for Oliver to take it. Oliver takes the overcoat from Jack, who is up against the closed window now with his hands in the air triumphantly. He's lapping up the attention from outside while shouting 'Jackpot' repeatedly. The crowd is waving and cheering. I'm staying away from the window. I can't see them, but you can be sure Sandra and Michael are still out there.

I'm getting uncomfortable. This is getting out of hand. I need to bring things to a conclusion, then get out of there as soon as possible. Edward looks like he is feeling the same; he turns to look at me again. I can see he has a bit of swelling around one of his eyes from when he bumped into the door. He goes to speak to me, but I get in before him.

"We're nearly done here, Mr Davenport." I say formally. "We appreciate your patience. Mr Potter and I just need a minute or two in private." I walk to the door and gesture for Edward and Oliver to leave the room. Edward and Oliver edge towards the door reluctantly. They keep a wide berth of Jack. Before they are out, Edward turns back to me and says.

"We didn't get your name yet, sir. You know there will be formalities to do, paperwork and that." I usher them both on out.

"Mr Potter and I have a few formalities ourselves. We'll be with you very soon." Oliver realises he's still holding Jack's overcoat. He's reluctant to go near Jack, so he hands it to me on his way out.

It's back to me and Jack in the room again. Jack is still at the window, lapping up the attention. I don't know Jack, but I figure he's a street-smart man but probably not a smart man. I have a figure in my head. An amount I think I should give him. My plan is to give Jack enough money so he will be more than comfortable for the rest of his life. What's in it for me? I can walk out of the lottery offices today anonymously and also knowing that no one will be looking for the winner of the Billion Euro jackpot.

Everyone wins with this plan. It will be easier for me to stay anonymous. Jack is broke; he'll become a wealthy man. The media and the world get their man. Even the lottery and Mr Davenport win. They want someone out there going public with this.

Jack will have to walk outside and say he won the Billion Euro. He already looks like he's getting used to that. He's loving the attention from outside. How much money does he think I will give him, though? Time to negotiate with him. I've decided to be fair. In my opinion, the figure in my head is more than fair. My magic number is the fair amount.

I call him over from the window. "Jack, Jack, we need to talk. You're getting ahead of things. We haven't come to our... How should I put it? We haven't come to our arrangement, Jack." He's in great form and swaggers over to me, as if he thinks that he's in charge of our arrangement.

I tell myself if Jack doesn't agree; I walk away. It will be as if the last hour didn't happen. I'll have my Billion Euro. I'll still be anonymous. This arrangement is on my terms or on no terms. I still have Jack's overcoat. He's all fidgety, flailing his arms around. So, I hold on to it for now.

"What do you think, Jack? How much do I need to give you for this arrangement to work?" Jack is straight back with an answer.

"I'll want a half pal or forget about it; won't take a penny less."

I'm deflated; I'm thinking I should have known. What was I thinking, anyway? There is no point trying to talk sense with someone like Jack Potter. I hand him back his overcoat. He takes it but can sense my mood change.

Does Jack really think I would give him half? Maybe my plan wasn't so good after all. I should get Edward Davenport back in here. Get the formalities done and get out and away as quickly as possible. Jack senses I'm not happy. He tries to push his offer. "Take it or leave it, pal. Give me half a million Euro, and like you said, you get to stay anonymous." This catches me off guard. He's looking for half a million. Not half of the Billion!

I'm back on track. I could have shaken Jack's hand there and then. It was the figure he suggested, after all. I could have given him what he asked for, followed on with my plan, and disappeared. No matter what I thought of this man, it wouldn't be a fair deal in my eyes. I'm going to be fair. The price I have in my head is the fair price, and that's what I'm going to offer Jack for his part in the deal.

"Jack, I'll be straight with you. I'm going to offer you what I consider is a more than fair price." Jack butts in while I'm talking.

"Listen, pal." I put my hand out and stop him talking.

"Let me finish, Jack. Trust me, you're going to want to hear what I have to say." I move over near the window and peek outside. "Jack, if you walk out of here, tell them you are in fact the Mega Millions Jackpot winner of one Billion Euro. I will give you five million Euro." Jack looks stunned. He's standing motionless, with his mouth wide open. Then he shouts out.

"Fuck this shit! Fuck this shit! Five million, five fucking million." He's jumping around the room now; he throws his overcoat up in the air and it ends up on the floor. I can see the door slowly opening behind me. I edge backwards and push it closed with the heel of my foot. I lean against the door with my back.

I watch as Jack dances a merry jig around the room. How have I ended up here? I've just offered a stranger five million Euro. I'm also feeling a sense of relief. It's a good deal all round. I'll be able to stay anonymous. I'm already giving this money away. I'm not collecting a Billion Euro now. I'm collecting nine hundred and ninety-five million Euro. Like I said, I didn't want to be a Billionaire.

I get Jack's attention. He almost seems drunk with joy and excitement. "Do we have a deal, Jack?" I step away from the door and offer my hand for him to shake, but he suddenly grabs me in a hug.

"Fucking deal, pal. It's a fucking deal. And call me Jackpot, you can call me Jackpot, pal." There's a knock on the door and it slowly opens. It's Edward and Oliver. They slowly step into the room. They both look confused and aren't sure what to make of things. Edward speaks,

"Like I said, gentlemen, we have some formalities to deal with. Are we all good here?" Jack is clapping and walking around the room like a peacock now. He stops and turns to Edward.

"Let's get this on. Where do I sign? Where do I get my fucking money?" Edward and Oliver are looking at me.

Looking for answers. They are wary of getting too close to the unpredictable Jack. I say to them,

"I think we're ready, gentlemen. You heard the man. What do you need us to do?"

"Great," says a relieved looking Edward. "We're moving to suite four. It's more comfortable there. Can you follow me please, gentlemen?" Edward walks out. Oliver gestures for me and Jack to follow. As we walk out, I pick Jack's overcoat up off the floor from where he threw it. I straighten it out and hand it to Jack. He takes his overcoat and we both walk towards the door. Jack then stops suddenly; he pauses while muttering to himself.

"Wait! Wait!" He suddenly shouts. He puts his hand across the doorway, stopping me from leaving the room. He rudely pushes Oliver ahead out of the room. He closes the door. It's me and Jack alone in the room again. I'm wondering if he's changed his mind.

"Is everything okay, Jack?" I say to him,

"Listen, pal." He says and then continues. "Nobody just gives me five million yo-yos. It's not right unless I give you something in return, pal. So, you understand. This is a business deal. That's how I roll."

I was confused. I didn't know what he meant. I could hear Edward and Oliver on the other side of the door. They were whispering. I couldn't hear what they were saying, but it was obvious they were more than a bit stressed, to say the least.

Jack holds up his overcoat. "This is all I had when I walked in here today, pal. I buy and sell stuff. That's what I do. I sort of bought this overcoat today." He pauses while he looks at the label on the inside of his overcoat. I'm puzzled. I don't know where this conversation is going. "How much will you give me for this overcoat, pal?" He then reads from the label on the overcoat. "This is the original Mack. Established in Glasgow in 1846. The Mackintosh overcoat. Often copied. Never equalled."

I couldn't figure out what he was doing initially. I was wondering if he had lost his mind. He was still holding the overcoat up. Moving it around at different angles for me to see.

"How much will you give me, pal? I need you to buy this overcoat off me." There was an uneasy pause as we both looked at each other. He's still holding it up, showing it to me. I then realise what he wants. He wants a business transaction. If it's important to him, I'll play along. He's just standing there waiting for an answer from me. Still holding the overcoat up with one hand.

"How about five million Euro Jack? Would you sell that overcoat to me for five million Euro?" That's all he wanted to hear. He's still dangling the overcoat up with one hand. He spits on his other hand and holds this hand out for me to shake.

"Deal," he says. I look at his spit ridden outstretched hand.

"Fist bump is the best I can do, Jack, under the circumstances, you know." The deal was done. With a fist bump.

Jack was ready now. We both were. He handed me the overcoat. No ceremonies or anything. He just bundled it over to me. The overcoat wasn't important to Jack. It was the transaction that mattered to him. I now own a new Mackintosh overcoat. Well, technically, it was second-hand. I'd just bought a second-hand Mackintosh overcoat for five million Euro.

Like Edward Davenport had said, there were formalities to be done. It was all done right and proper. Right to the point of not only had my ticket won the Billion Euro, but I also won a free scratch card on my other set of numbers.

Edward was all business, keen to get formalities out of the way. He was looking forward to getting out to the media. To get his photo taken. The interviews for television. This was his moment.

Oliver was particularly helpful to me. He advised me on sensible stuff. Like putting a list of family names on the ticket. He gave me good advice. Oliver didn't say it, but I suspect he knew what had been happening.

I watched as Jack Potter and Edward Davenport walked out of those glass doors to face the media and the crowd of people gathered outside. Edward's moment was somewhat ruined. He would have a black eye in the photographs after his encounter with the door. I was careful to stay away from the windows. I was still wearing my mask.

Sandra was front and centre, no surprise there. Michael was there taking photographs. There were about a dozen other reporters, along with a crowd of what looked like a couple of hundred people that had gathered. This was world news, after all. Since the Lottery draw was done, everyone wanted to know who won the Billion Euro. They had their man now. It was Jack Potter, and Jack was box office material for them all.

I didn't want to hang around. The reception area was chaotic. Staff were running here and there. Nothing like outside, absolute chaos out there. Jack was in the middle of it all and loving every second. I was back beside the reception desk. Just an anonymous guy. It was time for me to leave. I was still wary of being seen or having to explain why I was there to anyone. All eyes were on the man outside claiming to be the Billion Euro jackpot winner.

I had my new overcoat. I was thinking of Jack that morning and the way he wore the overcoat leaving the shop, trying to disguise himself with the collar up. I put the overcoat on and buttoned it up. I wasn't comfortable, so I took it off again. I decided I could hold it over my shoulder with one hand. I figured that this hand would also block some of my face. The chaos outside was to the right. Sandra had her back to me. I seized my chance.

Face mask on, holding the overcoat over my shoulder. I dashed out the door, turning left, away from the circus. The overcoat caught in the wind and flew back as I made my escape. It was like a cape. At least that's how it would look in the photograph. I was away down the road. Free and anonymous.

What I didn't know, in fact no one knew at the time; that precise moment was when the iconic photograph, 'Man with a Mackintosh overcoat,' was created. All my determination to avoid being seen by Sandra, I had forgotten about Michael. It was Michael who got the iconic photograph. He didn't know he had it. He didn't know the significance of that moment and that photograph. That will come later.

If the media storm surrounding the question of; 'Who won the Billion Euro jackpot?' was crazy; wait until the world goes looking for the man in that photograph; 'The man with the Mackintosh overcoat.'

Chapter 6

So, what are you supposed to do when you have just dashed out of the Lottery head office after claiming nine hundred and ninety-five million Euro? Not even that, you've just given a stranger five million Euro. You do what any normal person would do. You go for a pint.

I'm wondering and worrying about Jack Potter. Have I fed him to the wolves? He just got five million Euro. I believe he got a brilliant deal today. As he said himself, he had nothing walking in there except the clothes he was wearing and the Mackintosh overcoat. I could feel the adrenaline rushing through me, but I needed to just sit down. I needed to stop, get the face mask off, and take a breather. I needed to think things through.

A pub across the road caught my eye, The Crock Of Gold. It couldn't be more appropriate. Wouldn't do any harm to stop for one, take that breather. As I went to cross the road, a man caught my attention. He called after me, "Hey mister, you wouldn't have a spare Euro towards a hostel for the night?" It was Bruce and his dog, The Duke. I had occasionally given him the odd euro or two before. Here I am now; almost a Billionaire and I have no cash on me.

I was rummaging through my pockets; I was still holding my new overcoat. I was thinking of just giving Bruce the overcoat. He needed it more than I did, after all. He was standing there, waiting with anticipation.

"Sorry, I've no cash on me," I said to him. I was just about to hand him the overcoat when I found the lottery scratch card I had also won. "Here, take this, you might be lucky," I said to him while handing the scratch card over. He took the scratch card and tapped it gently on The Duke's head while saying,

"That's for luck between us, Duke." The Duke looked up at him ruefully, as if to say, 'Hopefully Bruce.'

"Listen," I said. "Where is this hostel? Let me pay for your hostel." He was looking at the scratch card, studying it.

"It's right there, buddy." He said, while pointing over his shoulder. Sure enough, we were standing right outside a hostel. It was a tall Georgian style building. It looked like it had seen better days.

"I'll go inside and pay for a room for you." Bruce was delicately scratching away on his scratch card with one of his fingernails. He didn't even look up at me.

"The name's Bruce; It's Bruce, and The Duke. They know us in there." I went into the hostel and paid for his room for a week. My first good deed. Not including what I did for Jack Potter, if you can call that a good deed. I looked around as I walked out. The place was dirty and badly in need of modernisation. I started thinking as I walked outside. There is no long term good just paying for one man's room. With all this money, I could buy the place. Make it respectable. Make a real difference.

Bruce was still scratching away on the scratch card when I went out. "That's sorted for you Bruce; you're paid for the next week." I said to him. "Good talking to you Bruce." He looked up from his scratch card briefly.

"Thanks, bud. You're a star, me and The Duke are grateful to ye." I headed across the road to The Crock Of Gold. I was almost at the door when I heard a shout from across the road. "Hey Buddy, you with the mack." I turned around to see Bruce dancing a little jig on the footpath. "Wa hoo! We won ten Euro," he shouted, while waving his scratch card around. I signalled thumbs up, then went on inside the pub. I needed a pint.

It was one of those deceptive pubs. A small front door, but when you walk inside, it's quite a big place. It was a traditional local pub. At least the clientele looked like they were locals. I find an empty bar stool near the service counter and sit down.

All eyes are on the three televisions scattered around the place. Did I really think I'd get a break from this? Jack Potter is on television. He's all over the news. The Mega Millions Jackpot winner has gone public. A few of the people in the pub seem to know him or know of him. There's great excitement but also a sense of disdain from some people. People who obviously know Jack in person. Maybe jealousy, or maybe they just know Jack too well.

Even the bar staff are glued to the news on the televisions. I manage to catch a barman's attention and order a pint. I'm relieved to have the face mask off, but I'm still holding the Mackintosh overcoat, which is awkward.

I see a coat-stand in the corner near the door. I go over and hang the overcoat there. I notice it's not the only overcoat hanging there. I sit down with my pint. At first, I was relieved to have gotten rid of it, but I can't relax now. It's too close to the door. I nearly gave it away to Bruce a few minutes ago. Now I'm worried it might get stolen. My being uneasy doesn't go unnoticed by a man sitting close to me at the bar.

Without looking up from his pint on the counter in front of him, he starts a conversation with me. "Don't worry, your coat is safe here. No one here will go near it." I was looking forward to just sitting on my own. I wanted to take stock of everything that had happened. I wasn't keen on talking to another stranger. I couldn't be rude, though.

"Ah. I know." I lie. "It's just that, well, it's sort of someone else's overcoat. I'm kind of minding it. I'm minding it for…." I pause. I was going to say, for a friend. Jack and I aren't friends. "I'm minding it for an associate of mine." The man just nods his head and goes back to drinking his pint.

All three televisions have the same channel on. There he was, Jack Potter holding a giant cheque for one Billion Euro. Posing for photos. Edward Davenport was all over the proceedings and with his shiner of a black eye, too. I couldn't see Sandra, but you can be sure she was still there.

When I say everyone was watching, I mean almost everyone. I couldn't watch anymore. I'd had enough. Someone else wasn't watching, though. My new pal on the bar stool isn't watching. He was just sitting there, shaking his head in disbelief.

He turns to me and says, "The entire world was waiting and wondering who won this. Hoping some good would come of it. Now we get this!" He points to one of the televisions without looking up, "and Jack Potter, of all people. I can't even look at him. It makes my blood boil seeing a man like him win all that money." He has my attention now.

"Who knows? Maybe some good will come of it." I say. He looks at me again, still shaking his head in disbelief and pointing at the television again.

"I know of Jack Potter, or Jackpot, whatever he calls himself. Trust me. No good will come of this. It would make you wonder about things, really." He takes a breath and a sip from his pint before continuing. "I mean, I'm not a religious man by any means, but if there is someone up there." He points up this time, as if pointing to the heavens. "He's messed it up big this time. He's really missed a golden opportunity to do a good deed here."

I was taking this man's comments personally for some reason. This guy did not know my plans. How could he know? Only I know about the good deeds planned with the money. I'm thinking it's time to go. Don't get involved. I hadn't intended on staying long, anyway. I had no intention of talking to a stranger either. I finish my pint quickly and prepare to leave.

It's time I got out of town. Get home. I want to phone Claire, and Jane. All this money and I suddenly feel overwhelmed. As I prepare to leave, He then says to me, "I couldn't help noticing you came out of that hostel across the road. Are you staying there?" I'm already on the way to the door and this question catches me off guard.

"No, I'm not." I say to him, "I'm actually thinking of buying the place." I was showing off now. He didn't reply, just nodded his head quizzically. I grabbed my overcoat from the coat stand. Turned back and said, "Nice talking to you. See you around," as I walked out the door.

I stood outside, looking at the hostel across the road. It looks old, but it's a fine building, four stories high. I wonder how many people could stay there and how many of them are in desperate circumstances. I'm also wondering how much a place like that would cost to buy. Does it even matter? I can afford it. This is one of the good things I could do. But I'm just a taxi driver. How would I go about buying a place like that?

The man I was talking to comes out of the pub. He sees me and says, "Thanks for minding my overcoat." I have my overcoat folded over my arm. Or what I thought was my overcoat. He has an overcoat in his hand. He's holding it up, smiling. I realise what has happened. I grabbed the wrong overcoat on my way out. I must have taken his overcoat. I'm so embarrassed.

"Shit, sorry about that." I say to him, The way I have the overcoat folded over my arm, stuff falls out of the pockets, a pen, and a few business cards. I quickly gather them up off the pavement. The man is sympathetic to my plight. Someone else could have misread this and accused me of stealing their coat.

"Don't worry about it," he says with a smile as we exchange overcoats. "My name's Austin, by the way; Austin Goodman." He puts his overcoat on. He's looking across the road at the hostel now and says, "I don't know if you were serious or not about buying that place over there." He points to the hostel. "If you are, I can help you. Or at the very least, I can give you sound advice."

He's going through his pockets now. At first, I thought he was checking in case anything was missing. I'm still standing there, embarrassed. He takes out one of his business cards and holds it out for me to take. "My number is on the back there. Call me if you need any advice."

I take the card from his outstretched hand. I'm looking at the card. Flipping it over, reading it. It's a standard business card. Goodman & Associates. Solicitors and Financial Advisers, has an address not far from here and a couple of phone numbers.

"I'm so sorry about the overcoat mix up." I stutter. I'm reading off his card now. "Mr Goodman," then add, "And you thought our coats were safe in there." He sees the funny side and offers his hand for me to shake.

"Please, my name is Austin. Call me Austin." We shake hands. I'm looking at the business card he has given me and looking across at the hostel. I'm thinking this might be just the man I need. I don't know him, but what's the harm in talking to him? Find out what he's about.

"Thank you, Austin." I say while still looking at his business card. "I might need a bit of advice, as it turns out."

"No problem. You have my phone number there." He says. He's pausing, then adds. "I didn't catch your name."

I'm pausing now, awkwardly. All day I've been doing my best not to tell anyone my name, trying to stay anonymous. Things are different now, though. The Billion Euro jackpot winner has been named, and it's Jack Potter. I look him in the eye and hold my hand out. We shake hands again.

"Sorry again about the mix-up with the overcoats, Austin. Thanks for being so understanding. My name is Billy…. Billy MacMann." Austin buttons up his overcoat. I put his business card in my pocket. "I'll be in touch, Austin." We said our goodbyes. I had a good feeling that this might just be the start of something, something good.

I had a couple of chance meetings today because of the Mackintosh overcoat. One chance meeting had ended with me buying the overcoat for five million Euro. This chance meeting with Austin Goodman was because of the same overcoat. I was soon to find out that Austin was, in fact, just the man I needed. Maybe that 'someone up there' he mentioned was listening after all.

I was exhausted now. I should be celebrating, but I needed to get out of the city. Get home and get things into perspective for myself. There was to be one more chance meeting regarding the overcoat. I had it draped over my arm. I was looking up and down the road for a taxi to get me home. A group of three young lads walked past me. They were probably about seventeen or eighteen years old. I should have been more alert and on my guard.

One of them grabbed the overcoat. Suddenly, the three of them were surrounding me, but they weren't threatening. They were having a laugh at my expense. The lad who grabbed my overcoat threw it over my head to his pal behind me, then he threw it to the third lad.

Next thing, a police car came around the corner, the three of them scarpered. They still had my overcoat. The police car drove on obliviously. I could have stopped the police and told them what had happened, but I wasn't really bothered. I didn't need any more hassle; I just wanted to get home. The overcoat was gone, stolen. I was more annoyed with myself for not being on my guard. My thoughts were, 'good riddance to it. Let any bad luck go with it.' I got a taxi and went home.

I was just relieved to be home. I was mentally and physically exhausted after the day's events. The house was empty. Claire should be here. Have I blown it with her? I'm wondering if I should phone her. I phone Jane, to see how she's doing.

Jane was not in good form. In fact, she was in a foul mood. Her mother and Michael were in town getting the news on the 'Mega Millions Jackpot Winner.' This meant they left Jane at home minding her younger brother and sister.

It was a short conversation with Jane, but I was just delighted to hear her voice. "Hi Jane, how are you getting on?"

"Fine, Dad," then adding," I can't talk for long. I don't have much credit on my phone." I can take a hint.

"Ok, Jane, no problem. I was hoping to meet you tomorrow. In fact, I'm going to buy you a new phone. How does that sound?" She was all ears now.

"Oh, oh great! Are you sure Dad? Thanks Dad, what time can you collect me?"

We arranged that I'd collect her at about eleven in the morning. I hadn't seen her for a few days, so I was looking forward to it. I also felt great that even if she didn't know it yet; she was set up for life; she'd never have to worry about money, or phone credit, ever again.

I was in better form myself now and still wondering if I should phone Claire to see where the land was with us. See if I've blown my chances. I'm also wondering if Claire has blown it. I mean, I miss her, and I really want to share this news with her. The thing is the last few phone calls we had; she hung the phone up on me. Maybe it's Claire's turn to do a bit of chasing for a change. Or maybe I'll phone her tomorrow.

Chapter 7

It's the day after I collected almost one Billion Euro. I should be on top of the world, but I feel somewhat empty. I thought with collecting the money, all my worries would be over. Not even that; With Jack Potter claiming to be the Billion Euro winner, it meant I wouldn't be constantly looking over my shoulder. All the heat was on him now. I should have no worries. Here I am on my own, alone. I should have Claire here with me. I need Claire with me!

I leave the house and go to get in my car, forgetting to make sure the coast was clear. Mrs Fogarty is across the road. I wonder, has she been waiting for me? She's in her front garden, giving instructions to Mr Fogarty, who is busy working in the garden. He has garden shears in his hands. I can imagine what he wants to do with them as his wife barks instructions to him.

Mrs Fogarty sees me before I get to my car. Before I know it, she's over across the road like an excited child. She has been waiting for me. My first instinct is that she somehow knows about me winning the Billion Euro. She couldn't possibly know, of course.

I get my spoke in first and try to nip the conversation in the bud. "Good morning, Mrs Fogarty, I'm actually in a bit of a hurry. How are you this morning?" I say. Mr Fogarty raises his head from the garden across the road, wearily. Looks like he's glad of the break from his wife. I give him a wave and he waves back, then pretends to look busy.

"Hello Billy, nice day, isn't it?" Before I could answer, she quickly adds, "and how is Claire?" I didn't want to be rude.

"Claire is great." I tell her, "I'll be talking to her later, Mrs Fogarty. I'll tell her you were asking for her. I'm in a bit of a hurry now." I quickly opened my car door and was just about to get in.

"So, Claire got on okay at the Doctor's yesterday then?" she says quizzically.

She caught me off guard with this question. I couldn't hide it either, and she knew it. I was halfway in the car but turned and got out again. I'm thinking, panicking a little, Claire was at the doctors! Why didn't she tell me? Maybe.... maybe she tried to tell me on the phone yesterday. Is Claire alright?

Mrs Fogarty was standing there with a smug smile on her face. I was lost for words. I just wanted to get away from her prying eyes so I could phone Claire, make sure she was okay. "I'm sure Claire is fine, Mrs Fogarty. Thanks for your concern." I got in my car quickly and drove off.

Mrs Fogarty looked on with her smug smile as I drove away. I take my phone out of my pocket and phone Claire as I drive. The phone rings out and goes to voicemail. I hadn't prepared to leave a voice message. I was flustered and worried. I stutter a message. "Hi Claire, it's me, Billy... I was just wondering how you are.... actually, Claire.... I'm on my way; I'm on my way over to see you now. I hope you don't mind. Phone me Claire.... please phone me when you get this message. Thanks."

I had one eye on the road and the other on my phone, hoping for Claire to phone me back. I reason with myself as I drive. If there was anything serious Claire would have told me, she was seen at the doctors. It's not like she was seen in an ambulance. Could be a simple cold or something. Why didn't she answer her phone, though? My phone then rings. It's Claire. I pull the car over and answer the call.

"Claire! Great to hear from you. How are you, Claire?" I was relieved to hear from her. In fact, it was just great to hear her voice.

"Hi Billy, I got your message. I'm not actually at my parents' house right now." I didn't want to mention her being seen at the doctors. She was well enough to talk on the phone. It would be better if I could meet her. Then maybe bring it up if she didn't mention it.

"Claire, could we meet today sometime? I'd love to see you, we need to…. Clare, we need to talk."

"Yes, Billy, we could meet later today. That would be nice."

"Great Claire. Maybe we could meet for lunch? I'm seeing Jane this morning; I could meet you afterwards; at about one o'clock? I could pick you up at your parent's house. Is one o'clock good for you?"

"That sounds good, Billy; see you at one o'clock then. That's a date."

I felt much better after the call. Not even that, Claire said it was a date. We were going on a date, which was encouraging. Claire sounded good. We'll meet as planned now; I'll find out how she is, and how we are, I suppose.

I get a text from Jane. Her mother was going to town, so Jane had a lift in. We could still meet at eleven, but now we were meeting in the city. Now we were meeting at the phone shop. Jane meeting me in town, and at a phone shop, meant two things. She had a new phone picked out, so that's fine. The fact Sandra was giving her a lift into town suggested that Sandra was more than likely following up on the Jack Potter story.

I couldn't resist putting the radio on as I drove to town. Sure enough, the news was dominated by Jack Potter, the Billion Euro winner. It was huge news, after all. I was grateful that it was him in the news and not me. I was a little nervous too. Jack doesn't know who I am, but I was still depending on him to keep our arrangement quiet all the same.

I parked the car in town, close to the address on Austin Goodman's business card. I couldn't resist having a peek. At least I knew it was a real place now. The sign above the door reads, 'A. Goodman & Associates' in large bold writing. Then underneath in smaller text, 'Solicitors, Estate Agents & Investment Specialists.'

There was a shop across the road, and my curiosity got the better of me. I had to see what the newspapers were saying. I wandered inside the shop. What a shock I got; it was front page of all the newspapers. I shouldn't have been surprised, but it did shock me. Seven or eight different newspapers and all of them had headlines relating to Jack Potter and the Billion Euro Jackpot. Most had Jack holding the giant cheque. Edward Davenport managed to get his mug in a couple of them, too. There were a few sub headlines relating to Jack potter's criminal record.

I decided to buy the Dublin Today paper. Sandra and Michael work there. I was interested in reading what Sandra had to say about it all. Sandra didn't hold back in her article. She pretty much had the same attitude as Austin Goodman. As in why, of all the people in this world, had Jack Potter won a Billion Euro? She didn't doubt that he had won, mind you, just doubting that any good would come of it.

Sandra Birch and Jack Potter had history. Sandra knew Jack's character from her work writing about Dublin. She was aware of his criminal activities and that he probably wasn't the type of guy you would want to bump into in town.

It wasn't just the front page. It was pages two and three as well. Sandra listed his various criminal convictions, mainly petty stuff like theft and fraud. Not very flattering for Jack, but I doubt he would have been bothered. I imagine he would even be proud of his criminal record.

There were more photos inside, too. One photo in particular caught my attention. It was a photo of Sandra, microphone in hand, talking to Jack Potter. I was in the background of the photo. You couldn't make out it was me, but I knew. It was the moment I had left the Lottery head office. I tried to put it out of my mind but wondered were there more photos I might be in?

There was a television hanging from the ceiling in the shop for customers to see. The news channel was on. This wasn't just happening in Dublin, or Ireland, for that matter. The news was showing various newspaper headlines from around the world. The Irish man that won a Billion Euro, Jack Potter, or Jackpot, he was everywhere now.

The New York Times led with 'Jackpot! Lucky Irish Man Scoops One Billion Euro.' It also had a bizarre photo of an Irish Leprechaun, but they had photoshopped it to look like Jack. Even as far away as Australia, The Australian People newspaper had a photo of Jack with the headline, 'Crikey, You Lucky Blighter Mate.'

I wasn't really surprised. It was to be expected after all the hype leading up to the Mega Millions Lottery and the 'who won it' questions afterwards. It just seemed so real now. This was the reason I did the deal with Jack Potter. Wasn't everything going according to plan? I was the anonymous winner of one Billion Euro. Jack takes all the publicity and was rewarded by becoming a very wealthy man. I imagine Jack would love all the attention around this. He was the main man in town now.

This will be hot news for a few days, and then blow over. Jack Potter will still be a wealthy man. I'll still be anonymous, and I won't be looking over my shoulder, because the media got their man. They have Jack Potter.

I can get busy giving this money away now. I have my list to start with. I have a gut feeling that Austin Goodman will be of significant benefit to me. Not even that. I have a date with Claire later. Things are looking good, but I just can't get that photograph in the newspaper with me in the background out of my mind.

I was all set now to meet Jane. I was looking forward to just seeing her. I wouldn't be able to tell her; at least not yet anyway, that she was set up for life now at only sixteen years of age. All my family would be. My brother and sister, and their families. Claire too, and all of her family.

I walked around to meet Jane at our designated meeting point, the phone shop. As delighted as I was to see her, all I could see was the tee shirt she was wearing. I couldn't believe it. Jane had a new tee shirt with a new slogan; 'Jack Potter Is My Sugar Daddy.' I couldn't look past it.

Hugs and kisses, but the tee shirt! It took me by surprise. Then again, it could have been worse. At least the name 'Billy MacMann' wasn't on the tee shirt. The slogan could have and maybe should have been, 'Billy MacMann is My Daddy.' If Jane only knew the day I had yesterday.

Jane was in great form; she was hyper excited and why not? She was seeing her dad! Well, the reality was, Jane had her eye on a snazzy new phone. She's a typical teenager who likes to have the latest fashions and gadgets. She's also a typical teenage daughter. She was well accomplished at pushing her dad's buttons to get what she wants. Truth is, I would give her anything she wanted; and now I can.

Jane hemmed and hawed in the phone shop. She was hovering around one particular phone. It was expensive. "Oh, look Dad. That's the same one my friend Jennifer has," she hinted, while trying to gauge my reaction. I gave her the standard shocked Dad reaction. Jane let out a sigh and edged towards the next phone at a slightly lower price range while gauging my reaction with a sidewards glance.

I pointed to the latest top of the range and probably the most expensive phone. "What about that one, Jane? It's only one hundred and fifty Euro" I said, playing the standard dumb old Dad routine.. Jane looked at me in shock this time.

"Dad!…. That price is not one hundred and fifty Euro, it's one thousand five hundred Euro!"

I have spent less money buying second-hand cars over the years. I bought the phone for Jane, because I could. Why not? I may well be giving most of this money away, most of it! I'm still going to be a very wealthy man.

Still in shock, Jane was delighted. She couldn't thank me enough. "Wow, Dad! Have a look at the camera on this! I'll be able to make better TikTok videos."

Once Jane had her new phone, I knew she was keen to meet up with her friends. She needed to show it off, along with her latest fashion tee shirt. She was too nice to say it, but I can take a hint. I let her get on with it. Besides, I was meeting Claire in about an hour. We had a date!

There's a bit of a scrum of reporters and gawkers down the road outside The Grand Hotel. I can see Sandra is there, along with other reporters. I can guess that Jack Potter is staying in that hotel, and why not? He's a wealthy man now. Good luck to him as far as I'm concerned.

I figure that if I had claimed that money anonymously, like I planned, there would be a hunt for the winner this morning. Instead of Jack Potter on all the newspaper headlines, it would be a question of; who claimed the Billion Euro jackpot? They have their man now in Jack Potter. Time for me to go. I have a date, a date with Claire.

Chapter 8

I was looking forward to meeting Claire, to just seeing her. She sounded good on the phone, but I was worried that everything was okay with her after the doctor's appointment. I was also worried that everything was okay between the two of us. I pretty much have all the money in the world, but it's no good without Claire, or if she has a serious illness.

I arrived a few minutes early. Claire opened the front door while I was parking outside the house. I was nervous; it felt like our first date again. Claire walked to meet me at the car. She seemed happy to see me. I sensed things were going to be good for our date.

We hugged, which eased the tension instantly. In fact, I almost, right there and then, told Claire about the Billion Euro but held myself back, held my nerve. Let's see how she is first, and then see how we are. Claire looked well, in fact she looked fantastic. Not like someone who had been to the doctor's the day before.

"Great to see you, Claire. You look well." I hinted. I quickly realised my mistake, then added, "Claire, you look fantastic. Where shall we go for lunch?" Claire smiled.

"Let's go into town, Billy, see where we end up." She turned around and realised her mother was standing at the front door of the house. Her mother was looking out, smiling. One of those 'ah, isn't that lovely' smiles that only mothers give. I waved to her.

"Hi Collette, it's good to see you." This was like a starting gun for her to get moving from the door. Before I knew it, Collette had marched straight over to me and given me a big hug. The hug was well received. It just caught me off guard. Collette finally released me.

"Ah, Billy, great to see you. You know you're always welcome here." She then looked at Claire but said to me, "No matter what that moody cow says." Claire just smiled and threw her eyes up, as if to say, 'mind your own business.'

Collette gave Claire an equally big hug and jokingly told her to be nice. Claire and I got in the car; we had a lunch date. We swapped a bit of small talk. Claire asked all about Jane, and my brother and sister. We were getting on great. Before we knew it, we were in town parking the car.

We were going for lunch, and with no particular place in mind, we just walked for a while and talked for a while. We talked things through, and we both apologised to each other. I took a chance and held her hand as we walked. Claire didn't resist. It was almost like old times again. She hadn't mentioned her doctor's appointment at this stage. I decided to wait a while, to see if she mentioned it rather than asking her. I so wanted to tell Claire of the events yesterday, tell her we were sorted, much more than sorted.

Somehow, we ended up outside The Crock Of Gold pub and decided to have lunch there. We were shown to seats near the back, where there was an area for patrons who were dining. We were barely sitting down when I couldn't hold it in any longer. I needed to tell her about the Billion Euro. She had to be told. I had to tell someone. Not someone. I had to tell Claire. I should have told her earlier.

I took a deep breath. "Claire, I've something to tell you…. I should have told you earlier…. I just didn't know how." I was stuttering now. "I just couldn't…. the way things were and all…. you know." I probably sounded too serious, and Claire looked at me with a concerned expression. I put her at ease. "No, it's good news Claire, brilliant news, in fact." My hand was resting on the table; Claire put her hand over mine. I sensed she was nervous; we both were.

"It seems we both have good news, Billy; I have news for you, too." Just then, there was a bang and a clatter as the door swung open at the pub entrance. Everyone in the place turned to see what was happening. A gang of about a dozen people noisily thundered in. They were loud and excited. It was Jack Potter, and a group of his friends, or a group of hangers on.

He had his arms up in the air triumphantly as he approached the bar counter. "Jackpot, everyone! I'm Jackpot, the drinks are on me." He turned to one of his friends and barked, "Macker; mind the fuckin door, don't let any of those nosey fuckin reporters in here. Understand? Keep those fuckers outside, Macker."

Jack Potter was in a great mood, they all were. The scene reminded me of the day before, when the security guard McGrath got Jack into the lottery head office and wouldn't let the reporters in. Now it was Jack in a pub and his pal Macker not letting the reporters in.

Everyone knew who he was by now. People clapped and cheered. I even found myself clapping and cheering. I was delighted for him. Why shouldn't he be out celebrating? A few reporters were outside. Macker on the door, holding a pint of beer now, wouldn't let any of them inside.

I noticed Claire wasn't clapping or cheering; she was just looking over, taking everything in. The waitress arrived with our food and placed it on our table. "You know who that is, don't you, Claire?" She was still looking over at Jack Potter and the crowd of hangers on around him.

"Everyone knows who he is, Billy. He's been all over the news, and now he will always be looking over his shoulder." Claire paused, and then added, "I think he's a very foolish man, Billy."

"Ah Claire, what harm is he doing? Sure, isn't the man celebrating? He got five million Euro yesterday." Claire looked over at the group. They all had drinks and were ready to party by the looks of them.

"Billy, that's the man who won a Billion Euro!" I realised my mistake.

"One Billion, that's right Claire, one Billion Euro."

"I think he's a very foolish man Billy, he shouldn't have told anyone." She paused, and then continued, "If it were me, I would have stayed anonymous, collected the money, and not told a soul. Would you just look at all those hangers-on around him? And that crowd outside? He's being followed by reporters, Billy. That man will have no peace." I couldn't help probing a little now.

"Maybe you're right Claire; he probably should have kept it quiet…. and maybe just told his family, I suppose." Claire was still looking over at the shenanigans around the bar area.

"Yes, Billy, that's what I would have done. Kept it quiet, told my family, maybe a couple of close friends." She turned and looked at me. "Now, never mind him. Tell me, Billy, what's this big news you have for me?"

I steadied myself. How do you tell someone you've won a Billion Euro? I took a deep breath, but before I could talk, Claire interrupted me. "You know what, Billy? The more I think about it, I don't think I would tell my family." She paused while she was thinking to herself, then added, "I would tell them eventually, just…. just not straight away." This stopped me, unsettled me, so I probed further.

"What do you mean by eventually, Claire?" She was looking over at Jack Potter and his hangers on again.

"I think he should have collected that Billion Euro anonymously, Billy, then waited a while, let things settle down. Have a…. how should I put it? He needed to take a cooling-off period, Billy. It's a life-changing event for everyone involved. In a week or so, this won't even be news anymore. Then he could tell his family." I couldn't resist probing even further.

"You'd tell me, wouldn't you, Claire?" She looked away from the events around Jack Potter. She took my hand and looked at me now.

"Of course, Billy. You would be the first person I would tell." This put me at ease. I took a deep breath again and prepared to tell her about the Billion Euro. Claire was in deep thought. "Actually, Billy, the more I think about it, I wouldn't tell you straight away. It would be after the cooling-off period, after I had time to get my own head straight. Now, enough of this silly nonsense. We both have good news. You go first."

Claire was right. The cooling-off period made perfect sense. Let the dust settle for a while. Here she was now, waiting for my big news. Jack Potter and his cronies were getting louder at the bar; there were a few reporters at the door demanding to get inside. Macker at the door was still holding firm. Claire was waiting for my good news. I had good news for her.

"Claire," I paused, "I hadn't told you; you know, the way things have been lately. It's just that…. well…. It is good news, Claire. We have a confirmed date for my mother's celebration. My family are all coming home next week. We're going to celebrate Mum's life properly." Claire smiled wryly.

"Billy, I know all about it. I do talk to your sister, and your brother, despite, as you put it; the way things have been. This is great news, Billy. We all miss her and it's great that we can all finally celebrate Angela's life." She paused for a few seconds. She seemed nervous, anxious, then continued.

"Besides, with everyone home, it will give us a chance to tell them our good news, Billy."

"Our good news, Claire?" I said quizzically. She was still holding my hand; she placed my hand on her tummy.

"Billy, we're going to have a baby. The doctor confirmed it yesterday." I was speechless, delighted, but lost for words. I just hugged her and managed to say,

"A new baby, our very own baby. This is just the most fantastic news ever, Claire."

What a date it turned out to be. Claire and I had put our differences the previous week or so behind us. We were planning for the future now. We even talked about planning a new date for our wedding. All good, and I still hadn't even told her about the Billion Euro. Not even that, when we went to pay for our lunch, we were told everyone's bill was being paid by their guest at the bar, Jack Potter.

As we were leaving, I suddenly realised that we would have to walk past Jack Potter on our way out. I didn't want to get too close in case he recognised me. I looked for the best possible route out where we would be as far away as possible from him. Jack's gang had grown considerably. Jack was in the middle of it all with wads of cash, which he was handing out like confetti.

Claire and I linked arms as we walked out. I had a safe, or safeish, route in mind and went for it, unconsciously hurrying Claire along. But Claire had her own route in mind. She was headed towards Jack Potter, not away from him! Claire dragged me along her route. I panicked. "Claire! Where are you going? What are you doing?" Our arms were linked, and I found myself being dragged towards Jack Potter rather than away from him.

"Billy! That man has paid for our lunch. The least we can do is thank him. I don't care who he is or how much he won. It's common manners to thank people, Billy. We need to say thank you to him."

I felt like a bold child as Claire led me along. She stopped just a few feet away from Jack Potter. Claire didn't say anything, she just looked at me as if to say, 'there you go Billy, what have you got to say for yourself?' I didn't look him in the eye, just shouted over, meekly,

"Thanks Mr Potter, thanks for buying our lunch." Hearing his name, Jack turned to face Claire and me. He had a pint of beer in his hand, he raised it in the air as if to 'cheers' towards us and said,

"Jackpot! The name's Jackpot, folks." He then carried on celebrating with his cronies. He didn't recognise me; he'd never seen me without the face mask on. I was anonymous to him.

We got out past Macker on the door; a few reporters tried to get in. Macker wouldn't budge. I got unnerved by a group of teenagers waiting up the road. I couldn't be sure, but they looked like the three lads that had grabbed my overcoat the previous evening. It was the man across the road that grabbed my attention, though.

It was Bruce. The Duke was with him, standing patiently at his side. They were standing outside the hostel. Bruce gestured for me to go over to him. I was wary of the three lads. I kept one eye on them and held Claire close to me as we crossed the road.

Bruce looked nervous. "Is everything okay, Bruce?" I asked. He was nervous; nervous, angry, and embarrassed. Bruce leaned in closer to me and said,

"Wait there, Buddy, just wait there for me." He disappeared into the Hostel, then came out holding an overcoat in his hand. It was my Mackintosh overcoat. He handed me the overcoat without saying a word.

He looked up the road at the three lads. He gestured to them with a casual wave of his hand. They immediately walked over to us while doing their best to avoid eye contact with me. They just looked down at the ground casually, hands in their pockets. I recognised them, though.

Bruce addressed them sternly. "Stand up straight lads, show some respect." The three of them immediately stood straight and took their hands from their pockets. You could tell they respected Bruce.

Bruce looked at the three of them with a stare, as if he could cut them in half. He grabbed the sleeve of the lad closest to him. "This is Maurice. He's a nephew of mine, he's usually a good lad, they all are…. Usually!" He let go of Maurice's sleeve and pointed at the other two. "That one there, with the curly hair. His name is…. that's Curly. We just call him Curly, and the tall lanky one is Larry; Lanky Larry."

He then looked at me and Claire and continued. "These three numskulls should know better, too. They're good lads, but they just let themselves down yesterday, and they let me down." Bruce paused for breath. You could tell how disappointed he was with the lad's behaviour. "What do you say to the man? What have ye got to say for yourselves, lads?" With that, the three of them turned towards me, and, almost in harmony, said,

"We're sorry, mister, we meant nothing by it." Before I had time to acknowledge them, Bruce had raised his hand dismissively, and they were gone, running off down the road. I had my overcoat back.

"Thanks Bruce. I can see that was hard for the boys, and for you. Bruce, if you need anything, just let me know." He looked me in the eye. You could tell he was angry with what had happened.

"No, Billy. If you need anything, you let me know." He meant it too. I thanked Bruce for my overcoat, myself and Claire carried on down the road. I had the overcoat in one hand and held Claire's hand with the other.

"What was that all about, Billy? And the overcoat? Is that.... Is that yours?" I wasn't sure how to answer Claire. I gave her a brief explanation of how I had bought the overcoat the day before. The three lads took it as a joke and now.... well, now I have it back. I didn't say who I bought it off. Claire didn't ask me how much I paid for it.

Claire suddenly stopped walking and just stood there, looking at me. "Well? Go on then, give us a look, give us a goo." I didn't know what she meant. She pointed at the overcoat. "Put it on Billy; give us a look at your new overcoat." I reluctantly put my overcoat on, right there and then on the street.

She stepped back and took a hard look at me. She then stepped towards me and buttoned up the overcoat and straightened the collar. She stepped back and took another look at me. "Yes, I like it. It suits you, Billy MacMann; You look like a million dollars."

Claire and I walked and talked for a while. I found it almost impossible not to tell her about the Billion Euro. I said to myself that after my family came home for our mother's celebration, I would tell Claire then, and tell my family. That seemed like a reasonable cooling-off period, as Claire had called it.

We'd been through so much the previous year; it was time to look to the future now. Our new baby was due in July. We also had a wedding to plan, or re-plan. We decided to get married in March, ideally in and around the same date we were supposed to get married last year. Not even that; We had all the money we could ever spend, and more. Claire didn't know this part yet.

When we arrived back at Claire's parents' house, Collette was at the front door to greet us. It was almost like she hadn't moved since we left a couple of hours earlier. I suppose she was nervous about how our date would go, too. She had another one of those broad mother smiles when she saw us.

Things were great now. Claire was moving back home. Collette cooked us dinner and invited Jane, too. Jane's latest tee shirt had an unflattering photo of Jack Potter on the front with the slogan, 'Jackpot- All The Pot In The World.'

Everything was great and I hadn't even arranged to meet Austin Goodman yet. So, things would get better still.

I phoned Austin Goodman the following morning. He remembered me; we arranged to meet at his office that afternoon. I dressed up for our meeting. I even wore my Mackintosh overcoat. The overcoat cost me five million Euro after all. I wanted to get some value for my money. Besides, as Claire said, 'I looked like a million Dollars.' I was about to give away millions and millions of Euro.

Chapter 9

I met Austin Goodman at his office in town. As far as I was concerned, this was a 'get to know you and see what you're all about' meeting. I was wary of giving too much information away at this stage. After initial formalities, the weather, the sports results, and we joked about the overcoat mix up; we sat down to talk business.

I had a cover story to begin with. I explained to Austin that my mother had passed away and my brother and sister were coming home next week. I gave the impression that our mother's estate was being settled, including selling the family home. We now had money we wanted to invest in the future. I didn't say how much money, Austin just nodded as I talked. My story was plausible, after all.

His office was tidy, with everything in its place. You would expect to see the usual business-related pictures or diplomas hanging on the wall, or even family photos. Not here in Austin's office. He was a bit of a nerd for movie memorabilia and comics. He had old posters and photos all over his office. Not just any old memorabilia, either. This was all superhero memorabilia, but nice stuff. I'd say a lot of it was original, maybe even worth a few quid.

He had Batman alongside his nemesis; The Joker, the original ones, from the nineteen sixties. Superman was there with Lex Luthor. There were plenty of others and I can't say that I would have known them all. It was like Austin's office was a man cave for him, except it looked good. It was tidy and somehow still felt like a professional business premises.

There was no one else there except the two of us. I had been wondering who his associates were from his business card and sign out front. 'A Goodman & Associates.' I asked him about it. Austin explained he was scaling down his business lately. He just had a secretary that helped him from time to time, and this secretary was his wife.

What impressed me most, though, was that he had done his homework. I had talked to him that morning to arrange the meeting. Austin had already found out information about the hostel. He was already on the case. He advised me that there might be another hostel near Temple Bar that might be a better investment. Austin suggested he could make enquiries for me. Maybe we could even play the two against each other regarding the price.

I knew of this place. It wasn't far from where my friend Kevin had his struggling restaurant business. This gave me an idea. I didn't mention Kevin, but I asked Austin to make enquiries about the restaurant premises, too. As you do, you know; 'while you're down that way, Austin.'

Austin might have been scaling down his business, but I was about to make him one of the busiest men in Dublin. Dublin would be the better for it too. Not just Dublin, I had ideas beyond Dublin. Things were going to start happening. I had found the man outside my circle to help. We were going to make a great team.

We shook hands as I prepared to leave. I was looking around his office, at all his pictures and memorabilia. I could see that he noticed my interest. I got the impression he wanted me to ask him about them. I couldn't let him down.

"You have an impressive collection here, Austin." I said while looking around, and it was impressive to be fair. "So, tell me, which one is your favourite out of this lot?" Austin stood up from his desk.

"Oh, I don't know Billy, I can't say that I have a favourite, really. They all have different stories to tell." I was standing next to a framed Spiderman comic now and said,

"I always liked Spiderman myself. I always thought of him as a kind of one of the people, one of us, I suppose." Austin's eyes lit up now, delighted with my interest.

"The thing is, Billy, that there is one of my favourite comics. That comic is the first Spiderman comic, issue number one. I wouldn't like to tell you how much it's worth. Let's just say you could buy your hostel or that comic, Billy, but not both." He had a broad smile now as he continued talking. "Spiderman wouldn't be one of my favourite superheroes, though."

He then walked around his desk to the other side of his office. "The thing is Billy, most of these guys started as stories, or urban legends, if you like." Stories of normal people doing exceptional things. He pointed to one of the pictures I didn't recognise. It was a modern photograph of what to me looked like a woman in fancy dress for a Halloween party.

"You see her? That's Domestic Girl. She's a real-life hero in New York City. She advises and helps women who are suffering from domestic abuse." He then pointed to another photograph of a man with a red spandex suit and a yellow cape. "And this one here, he's a genuine hero too, Billy. This is Street Cred Man; he helps the homeless community in Chicago. There are no Hollywood movies about these two, but who knows? Maybe someday, that's how it generally starts, with real people making a real difference. Real heroes, Billy."

I left his office, Austin had work to do, and I could tell he was keen to get on with it. We agreed to meet again when he had gathered more information for me. Oh, and yes, I bought my mother's house. Simply, because I could. It was the family home, after all; I felt I had to buy it. My brother and sister didn't need to know who bought it, at least not for now, anyway.

Our Mother's estate was being sorted, including the house being sold. My brother, sister and I were getting a share. Not a life-changing amount, but enough all the same. Enough for me to explain to Claire how we could pay for our wedding. It might also help buy me more cooling-off time.

Chapter 10

I was kept well informed about what Jack Potter was up to. Everyone was the world over. He was constantly on the news. If he wasn't on the front page, he was somewhere in the news and social media every day without fail. Sandra was constantly writing about him, and Sandra was becoming a bit of a celebrity herself now, thanks to her own expertise on Jack Potter. All the media worldwide wanted to know everything about Jackpot, Jack Potter, so they talked to Sandra; the Irish expert on the Irish winner of one Billion Euro.

When I met Jack Potter at the Lottery head office, he told me he had just been through a divorce. The latest story is that Jack Potter's ex-wife is back on the scene. Seems that

Margaret Potter, better known as Peggy, has suddenly realised the terrible mistake she made by divorcing the now Billionaire Jack Potter. She doesn't know he's not a Billionaire. He's a wealthy man, nonetheless.

Front page of the news today, and all over social media, we have a photo of Jack Potter with his ex-wife Peggy. Jack had a look on him like the time I told him he was getting the five million Euro. Peggy had a look, and I suspect it was a permanent look. She looked like if you got on her wrong side, she would 'bleeden burst ye.'

They looked all loved up, and why not? They were announcing their engagement, or re-engagement, I suppose. They announced a date for their second wedding. Peggy and Jack booked their wedding ceremony in The Grand Hotel for the end of March. It was going to be a no expenses spared lavish affair. Jack and Peggy Potter were living it large now; they were staying in the Grand Hotel pretty much as permanent guests. It was one of the most luxurious hotels in the city.

Even Jane was making a name for herself with those silly tee shirts that were all the craze. I can't say that I know much about TikTok, but Jane showed me a few of the videos and photos doing the rounds, on her new phone fancy phone.

Jane had posted a few pictures and made a few videos. With her mother and Michael working on Jack Potter's story, Jane had the pick of all the latest photos of Jackpot. A few of her uploads even had over a thousand 'likes,' Jane boasted. It was all harmless fun, as far as I could see. The most important aspect, according to Jane, was that you wore one of the tee shirts mocking or laughing at Jack Potter. The cheesier they were, the better, and the more views and 'likes' she would get.

I was now the anonymous winner of one Billion Euro, or almost one Billion Euro. Nobody knew that I won. I had told no one, not even Claire. I was determined to give as much away as I could, to do as much good with the money where possible. I now had Austin Goodman on board to help me.

Let me tell you how a homeless man, his dog, and my fantastic daughter Jane inspired an anonymous donor to put free vets, doctors, and nurses on the streets to help the less fortunate.

The same anonymous donor was inspired to set up a scheme where two students from less fortunate backgrounds would get a fully paid veterinary scholarship for their studies at the hospital. I knew these particular students wouldn't forget their roots and would always give something back. There was likely going to be a positive kick back.

The same anonymous donor started the same scheme at the hospitals that trained student doctors and nurses. Good things were happening in Dublin and beyond. As it happened this day, Jane was in town looking for the latest tee shirt for her collection, and for TikTok. Jane phoned me. She was hysterical, frantic, and it really startled me.

"Dad, can you come into town right away?" I tried to calm her down.

"I'm on the way, Jane. Is everything alright? Where are you?" Her response surprised me.

"I'm okay Dad, it's not me, it's The Duke, there's something wrong with The Duke Dad, I think he's very sick." I didn't even know that Jane knew The Duke, and by association, she knew Bruce.

"I can be there in five minutes, Jane; where exactly are you now?" I needn't have asked. Bruce and The Duke had a regular spot at the top of Duke Street. Bruce occasionally sold some merchandise and was now selling the latest tee shirts. Jane was one of his best customers.

Anyone that knows Bruce knew he found The Duke behind the shops on Duke Street. The Duke had been rummaging for food around the bins. Bruce kind of rescued him if you like. I'm not so sure who rescued who or even which one of them was rummaging for food, but they've been inseparable ever since.

When I arrived on the scene, I saw Jane first; she was crying while frantically looking up and down the road waiting for me to arrive. Bruce and The Duke were both lying down on the pavement. The Duke seemed motionless, his tongue lagging out of his mouth. Bruce was lying down beside him and begging The Duke to stay with him. It was heart-breaking. I initially thought The Duke was already gone, but you could see he was trying to wag his stump of a tail every time he heard Bruce's voice.

A few of Bruce's friends had also arrived to help him or support him, even. They were other homeless people and with their help; we got The Duke into the back seat of my taxi. Bruce sat in beside his best friend. He had The Duke's head lying comfortably on his lap. Bruce was inconsolable.

Five minutes later, we were at the Veterinary Hospital. Another fifteen minutes later, The Duke was being prepared for emergency surgery. One hour and fifteen minutes later, the surgery was completed. The Duke was still sedated, but out of danger.

During this hour and fifteen minutes, the three of us waited anxiously for news. Bruce prayed to the heavens for the longest hour and fifteen minutes of his life. He couldn't sit still; he was distraught with worry. "What if The Duke doesn't make it? He asked. It was a question I was asking myself. What would he do without his constant companion, his best friend?"

I didn't sit still during this anxious wait, either. I went for a wander around the Veterinary Hospital. The hospital was also a training college for aspiring future Veterinary Doctors. I imagined maybe Jane might study there in a couple of years' time. I imagined it would be expensive to study there, but I didn't need to worry about expenses anymore.

As I wandered around, I checked on Bruce and Jane from time to time. It was heart-breaking to see the turmoil Bruce was going through while The Duke was in surgery. I was so proud of how Jane was handling everything, how she was helping Bruce through this. I suddenly didn't see my little girl anymore. This was a young, courageous woman.

Later that week, the Veterinary Hospital would have a visit from a man wearing a Mackintosh overcoat. He didn't give his name. The Veterinary Hospital would announce that an anonymous donor would pay for student Veterinary Doctors to run clinics on the streets of Dublin. Clinics where less fortunate people would get free care for their pets. This would prove so successful that they would roll it out to most cities in Ireland. Eventually, this would also be copied in hundreds of cities worldwide.

The Vet came out to see Bruce. She had good news. The surgery was a success. The Duke had suffered from 'a twisted gut.' He most likely would have died without the emergency surgery. For now, all he needed was rest, and they would keep him overnight for observation.

Bruce let out a heart wrenching sigh of relief. He was taken aback by all of this and couldn't believe how close he'd come to losing The Duke. Bruce had been on the streets most of his life and said nobody had ever shown him the kindness that Jane and I showed him; people he barely knew.

Bruce was told he could collect The Duke the following day. I paid the Vet bills. Bruce was in tears with emotion and relief at what had happened. He grabbed my hand and shook it with appreciation. He was trembling.

"Thanks Billy, I won't forget this." He looked at Jane. He had tears in his eyes, they both had. "And you, Jane, you're a legend for what you did, lass. You're both legends." He looked me in the eye now. He still had a hold of my hand. "I'll pay you back, Billy. I know a guy. I'll get the money for you tomorrow; I promise you that." I was just so relieved everything had worked out.

"Bruce, don't you worry about it. The main thing is The Duke will be back to himself soon. I owed you. Remember, it was you that got me my overcoat back. We're all good now. You just focus on taking care of The Duke." As we released our handshake, I slipped money into Bruce's palm. "Get yourself something good to eat. You need to mind yourself if you're going to mind The Duke now."

I offered to give Bruce a lift back to the hostel. He declined; he didn't want to be too far away from The Duke. Bruce stayed in the waiting room for as long as they let him. He spent the night in a doorway close to the Veterinary Hospital.

I drove Jane home. For once, Jane kept her phone in her pocket. We had a good chat. I was so proud of her. "Jane, you saved that dog's life today, and quite possibly Bruce, too. Who knows what Bruce would have done if he had lost The Duke today?" We talked about Jane's future. Maybe Jane would be a vet someday, I suggested.

"Maybe," she said. "Had I seen her latest TikTok video?" She asked.

"TikTok, Jane? You know I don't do TikTok. Can you send me a friend request?"

"Eh.… Ye.… sure thing, Dad!"

Bruce and The Duke were back on the streets in no time. The Duke had a nasty scar and had to wear one of those cones around his neck to stop him scratching for a few days. A homeless man with a sick dog gained a lot of sympathy on the streets; you couldn't blame them for taking advantage. They both ate well on the back of it.

The student vets started doing their rounds soon after, followed by student doctors and nurses. An anonymous donor set up more soup kitchens. The homeless and less fortunate were suddenly being looked out for now.

People were wondering why and who? All of this, and more, just started happening so suddenly. Nobody was taking the credit; even local politicians were baffled by it all. This all started not long after Jack Potter had claimed the Billion Euro jackpot. Naturally, people began to talk; was Jack Potter doing all of this?

Peggy, or Jack Potter's spokesperson as she was now, would regularly be asked if Jack Potter was responsible for the various anonymous good deeds that were happening. Her usual response was, "We will neither confirm nor deny that we're responsible."

I was a busy man. I had met with Austin Goodman again. Austin's plan to play both hostel owners against each other on price had paid off. Austin figured both were now available at what he considered a good price for property in the city centre. It was just a case of me and the family choosing which one we would invest in.

Austin suggested we should take time to think about it. I thought for about ten seconds while he sat opposite me. It hadn't occurred to me that I would have to choose one of the hostels. I instructed Austin to purchase both hostels at as good a price that he could negotiate.

He was taken aback by this but kept a cool professional demeanour. At the end of our meeting, I went to stand up and leave; then remembered. "What about the restaurant near Temple Bar Austin? Any updates on that yet?"

Austin explained the restaurant was under a long lease with a tenant who was on the verge of possibly being evicted. There were rent arrears issues. Austin suggested it was probably better to wait awhile on this property; maybe it would be better to wait until the trouble with the present tenant was concluded.

I instructed Austin to see if he could negotiate a fair price based on them dealing with the present difficult tenant. That's exactly what he did. Things were happening; and happening fast.

Within the next week or two, with Austin's expert work, I had bought two hostels, a restaurant and, of course, my late mother's house. I was investing wisely, too. These were all excellent investments.

Student Vets, Doctors and Nurses were helping the less fortunate. People in need were being fed at soup kitchens that were popping up around the country.

There was a house that Claire had always admired; it wasn't far from her parents' neighbourhood, so we had passed it regularly. I remembered Claire saying it was her dream house. I also remembered telling her, 'in your dreams sunshine,' whenever we happened to be driving past this particular house. I bought this house. I wouldn't be telling Claire yet. It would be a surprise for her, I could tell Claire after the cooling-off period.

I was spending millions, but I was spending it wisely. So many good things were happening. Austin Goodman was proving a great asset. We were becoming good friends, too. I was tempted to tell Austin about the Billion Euro. I felt I needed to tell someone. I decided to wait awhile; maybe till after the cooling-off period.

I also visited my friend Kevin at his restaurant. Kevin was still struggling and feeling the pressure. I arranged for Austin to meet Kevin, to advise him. I had concocted a plausible story with Austin where Kevin could stay rent free while the new landlord thought about redeveloping the premises.

The new landlord was going to take his time while he thought about redeveloping, so Kevin had no rent to pay. This was Kevin's lucky break. He turned things back in his favour again. Kevin never found out who his new landlord was.

I looked for a bounce back whenever I could, a positive kick back. I always looked at ways to get value for the money I was spending whenever possible. The only terms put to Kevin by his anonymous landlord, while he paid no rent, were that Kevin's restaurant would accept special food vouchers. The vouchers could be handed in by homeless and less fortunate people in exchange for a meal. This was all good for Kevin because he could redeem the vouchers in full. Business increased significantly for him because of this. These special food vouchers were handed out at the hostels and on the streets.

I bumped into the three numbskulls, as Bruce had called them: Maurice, Curly, and Lanky Larry. Didn't they owe me a favour now? I didn't take advantage. I paid them to distribute the vouchers responsibly on the streets. The three lads were game, and they got paid too. They wouldn't let me down; they knew they'd have to deal with Bruce again if they did.

Ace reporter Sandra Birch knew the three lads from around town. The lads were known in the city centre because they were rarely seen apart and were generally messing about. They mainly got up to harmless stuff like busking, break dancing and…. taking eejit's overcoats, I suppose.

The three lads called to see me. They wanted to have, as Maurice called it. 'A word in my shell like. A heads up.' I was all ears for what they told me. A nosey reporter, and I'm being diplomatic here, I won't say what they called her. A nosey reporter was asking questions about the food vouchers being handed out.

Maurice, Curly, and Larry are street smart. They wouldn't be keen on talking to nosey reporters. They wouldn't talk to anyone they didn't trust, but if you got them on your side, you had a friend for life. The numbskulls were on my side now and proved to be invaluable to me. They became my eyes and ears on the street. The lads knew Jack Potter, so I was getting information about his carry on from them, and from Sandra's regular news updates.

Maurice, Curly, and Larry didn't bat an eyelid between them whenever Sandra came asking questions. They met most of her questions with smart remarks or silly answers. The three of them just laughed and joked, much to Sandra's dismay. As far as the three lads were concerned; whatever happened on the streets was street business and nobody else's business.

Sandra even asked the lads if Jack Potter had anything to do with the vouchers. She quickly realised she would get no information or no sense from the trio, but there was another question she asked them which they wanted to tell me about. Sandra asked them if they knew anything about the anonymous man with the Mackintosh overcoat who was doing good deeds around town.

I was still wearing my Mackintosh overcoat as I got on with my good deeds and schemes. I wasn't doing all this alone. Austin Goodman was such a great help to me. He also had a similar overcoat to mine. Sandra was asking questions around town; she was told the good deeds were all done anonymously. Some people mentioned that the anonymous person was wearing a Mackintosh overcoat. With Austin and I both wearing Mackintosh overcoats; it must have seemed to Sandra that 'the man with the Mackintosh overcoat' was everywhere.

I had money, so I wasn't dealing with banks looking for loans. I was a cash customer. This, along with Austin being exceptionally good at his end, helped deals go through quickly. There was no time wasted getting the hostels up to standard either. Austin Goodman knew someone. A good operator who would do the renovations at a reasonable cost but to a high standard.

This was all done while keeping the hostels open. Not even that. I thought of a way to get another positive kick back. I insisted that a minimum of half the workers renovating the hostels had to be long term unemployed or homeless. Most of these workers ticked both boxes.

The hostels were free now for homeless and less fortunate people. As busy as I was, I was going to get busier. Busy with my family. It was just a few days before we were going to celebrate our Mother's life. I had two airport runs the next day.

My brother Martin was arriving in the morning from Chicago. Martin was bringing his wife and their three children with him. My sister Catherine was due to arrive a couple of hours later from New York. Catherine was bringing her partner and their two children. I had booked them all to stay, all expenses paid, at a luxury hotel in the City centre. My family were all staying in The Grand Hotel.

Claire and I were looking forward to seeing my family. We could tell them all about the baby and that we were going to rearrange our wedding. The wedding hadn't been booked yet, but we were hoping to confirm a venue for a March wedding. There was the other news! The nine hundred and ninety-five million Euro.

My so called 'cooling-off period' was ending. I still hadn't told anyone about the Billion Euro. Now that my brother and sister were on the way, it would be the perfect time to tell them and tell Claire. Was it the right time to end the cooling-off period, though? I was watching all the news about Jack Potter and how he was still being hounded all over the media.

I was enjoying doing all the good deeds while staying anonymous. I was even beginning to wonder if there was a way I could give family a share without telling them where it came from. Would I be able to carry on with all the good work anonymously if my family knew everything? Do I have to tell anyone?

I'm one of the richest people in Ireland. My happiness came not from what I had; it came from what I could give. I wanted to give more of this money away; I wanted to do all of this anonymously.

Chapter 11

I got up this morning and looked out the window. The Fogarty's new car has arrived and a few of the neighbours are out having a nose. Mr Fogarty was obviously impressed. He has a wide smile on his face as he stands staring at the car. He's scratching his head in bewilderment.

Mrs Fogarty is standing beside him, hands on her hips. She somehow looks both impressed and unimpressed at the same time; I can't hear what she's saying, but she's obviously giving Mr Fogarty a hard time. As if he's at fault somehow. He's not listening to her; he's too engrossed with the new car.

They will all be getting their new cars today. I ordered eight new cars, originally for people who helped care for my mother last year. Emma, who I gave a lift to a couple of weeks ago, will get her new car today. So will Mary and Noah, who worked at the nursing home and were particularly good to my mother. Doctor O'Sullivan too, my Mother's doctor, she's getting a new car today, they all deserve something in my eyes. The instructions were simple: that the cars be delivered with thanks, as a gift from an anonymous donor.

I hadn't forgotten about Benjamin, who made the ultimate sacrifice. Austin has been working away on Benjamin's case. Benjamin Abdullahi left behind his wife and three children. They live in a small village on the outskirts of Lagos, Nigeria.

I set in motion plans to build a school in his village and in his memory. The Benjamin Abdullahi School would be completed in a couple of months and would benefit everyone in his home village. Each member of Benjamin's family received fifty thousand dollars; all done anonymously with a simple message; Thank You.

I now had three spare new cars. I had a feeling that I might forget someone so intended to get an extra one; just in case, and just because I could. I even had an idea that I might give a random person a new car, simply because I can, and quite simply if I think they deserve it.

I hadn't intended to buy eight new cars. The salesman at the dealership naturally assumed I was looking to buy one new car. Things escalated quickly. When he realised that I might buy five or six new cars, he couldn't hide his excitement. The salesman made a phone call; his manager arrived pronto to join the negotiations.

They offered me discounts for this, add-ons for that. When they asked what type of finance I required, I told them I didn't need finance; I could pay in full that day. Things escalated again. The manager then made a phone call; the dealership owner arrived pronto to take over negotiations.

I hemmed and hawed. I was offered the sun and the moon. "Did you know I have another dealership where you could look at more cars?" He asked. This question got me thinking. Maybe I could get another positive kick back here. I had been offered the sun and the moon. I just needed the stars to be looked after.

I suggested I might buy more than my intended five or six cars. "I might take….. eight cars!" Negotiations escalated again. Before I knew it, I was offered discounts and add-ons with all sorts of bells and ribbons. The sun, the moon…. but not the stars for me at this stage.

When I said that, I would think about it; that maybe I'd check out the competition. I got what I wanted; the sun, the moon and the Stars were to be looked after.

Three young chancers were to be given a chance. The owner agreed to give Maurice, Curly, and Larry an opportunity to learn a trade at his dealership. A chance for them to become apprentice mechanics at his car service department.

The amount I spent on new cars would be silly money for any normal person. Not for me though. Eight people were going to get new cars as a thank you gesture. The kick back I got with the three lads getting an opportunity was especially sweet for me.

You might wonder why I gave the Fogarty's a new car. I've probably seemed a bit unkind when I've mentioned the nosey, gossiping, snooping Mrs Fogarty up to now. The Fogarty's were great friends of my Mother. They were particularly good when my mother was sick, and when my mother passed away.

Or maybe their new car was just a continuation of a gesture by my Mother from years gone by. I don't know if the Fogarty's knew where those secret envelopes came from. Maybe them being so good to my mother was a positive kick back. They don't know who bought them a new car and I couldn't fit it in an envelope.

A new car is a new car, but Mrs Fogarty didn't drive, so Mr Fogarty was the main benefactor of the car, really. I figured he also deserved the car, if only for having to put up with Mrs Fogarty. The fact that the car was a convertible

BMW seemed to grate with Mrs Fogarty. Maybe I should have known better; maybe I did know better.

Truth is, I was jealous of the new cars. I could have done with a new car myself. I'd have loved to be giving Claire a new car, and other people too, but I still hadn't told Claire about the Billion Euro. I hadn't told anyone.

We did get money from my mother's estate and that money was supposedly helping to pay for our upcoming wedding; so, arriving home with a new car at this point wouldn't be a good idea. As much as I'd like a new car, I figured I could wait until this so called 'cooling-off period' was over, and it was nearly over now.

When it was confirmed that family were coming home, the reality of the occasion hit me hard. We were celebrating our Mother's life, but the reality was we were giving her a proper send off. Our Mother hadn't been well, but we hoped she would improve. Then Covid took her from us.

I had been thinking about all the people who had been taken by the Covid virus. The casualty numbers were broadcast every day; these were not just statistics; they were real people; and families like my own left devastated at our loss. I decided to do something for the families, something in my Mother's name.

Almost fifty years ago, my parents, Angela and William MacMann were married at Saint Patrick's Church in the

Liberties part of Dublin. They celebrated the event in a small run-down hotel in the city centre. It was a small ceremony, by all accounts. Angela and William had a good marriage and were blessed with three children.

The same small run-down hotel expanded and modernised over the years. This hotel was now one of the most exclusive hotels in Dublin; 'The Grand Hotel.' I bought the Hotel. I bought the hotel in my parents' honour.

This, I can tell you, was a massive amount of money spent. It gave me great satisfaction to spend it though. The hotel was an investment on my part. I had a particular interest in the hotel gardens. There is no consolation to losing a loved one. I set in motion plans to build a garden of remembrance on the hotel grounds for victims of Covid. A peaceful place where families could go and remember their loved ones.

The next of kin of all victims in Ireland received a letter in the post. The letter simply stated that 'An Angel was looking over your dearly departed loved one.' There was legal stuff included in the letters. Victims' families were given permission to have a place to remember their loved one in the gardens. Effectively, they were all made joint owners of the Remembrance Gardens.

Don't get me wrong, I still owned the hotel. It was a property investment on my part. The letters were simply signed 'From An Anonymous Donor, Lest We Forget.' Only I knew who this Angel was. It was my mother, Angela. She was looking over me too. I felt she was even guiding me.

This was where Austin was again, so helpful to me. His part-time secretary was now working full time. Austin and his wife Sinead were flat out working for me and my projects. Sinead was as professional and efficient as her husband.

The thing about Austin was, he just got on with his work in a professional manner. He didn't ask me questions or question what I was doing. I wanted to tell him about the Billion Euro and would have told him if he asked. Austin is on my list. Austin and Sinead will be able to retire comfortably; they just don't know it yet.

There were so many good things happening in Dublin and beyond. So many things I haven't mentioned. There was the appeal on the radio, for example. An appeal went out to raise twenty thousand Euro to bring a seriously ill child to Disneyland. I sent Austin to the radio station with twenty thousand Euro.

Austin didn't just hand this money over. The premise was; if listeners raised twenty thousand Euro, I would match it with my twenty thousand Euro. So, in no time, forty thousand Euro went to the family. They could all go to

Disney and bring a few friends. Another positive kick back as I saw it.

There was also a special fund set up for families of front-line workers who were affected by Covid; it wasn't just money. Austin Goodman advised me to invest in property. He knew his stuff, too. The property was still in my name. Any income raised went towards these families.

Chapter 12

I have a busy few days ahead; Starting with two airport runs for my family today. My brother Martin and his family are due to arrive from Chicago at ten thirty this morning. My sister Catherine and her family arrive from New York at midday. Jane is coming with me, so I'll collect her on the way to the airport.

I check the flight information before I leave. It turns out my brother's flight is delayed and will be over an hour late. Looks like his flight and my sisters will arrive about the same time now. I text Jane with the update. Jane's reply, 'k,' is instantaneous. A minute later, Jane texts me again. 'How will they all fit in your taxi?' My almost instantaneous reply. 'I have that sorted, Jane. See you soon. XX'

This is where having a few spare BMW cars in a car dealers showroom comes in handy. Not even that, the same car dealer has three apprentice mechanics who I know very well. Maurice, Curly, and Larry borrowed a BMW each to help me with the family airport collections.

When I leave the house, I see Mr Fogarty sitting in his new car, which is parked in his driveway. He has the window down and he's resting his elbow on the open window frame. His other hand is on the steering wheel as if he is driving or imagining himself driving. He hasn't driven the car yet; I suspect he's a bit terrified. I can see Mrs Fogarty eyeballing him from inside the house. I suspect he's a bit terrified of going inside the house, too.

Jane and I wait patiently and excitedly at airport arrivals. There are lots of people waiting for loved ones to arrive; all craning their necks every time someone comes through the arrival's doors.

Catherine and Martin have made good lives for themselves in America. Big sister Catherine went to New York with her best friend, who is also named Catherine. We call her Cathy to save confusion. They're more than best friends and have a family of their own.

Catherine and Cathy have two children, two college highflyers: a daughter; Zoe, and a son; Ciaran. Zoe and Ciaran are both twenty years old, but they are not twins.

Catherine and Cathy just happened to be pregnant at the same time. I don't know how, and I didn't ask.

Catherine is the image of our dear Mother and has kept her Irish accent even after all these years. She is the eldest of the MacMann children. She's great fun, and a big softie at heart.

Next born, and living in Chicago, is our brother Martin. When Martin arrived in America, he never looked back. He has become Americanised. He even has an American accent. Martin is married to Melissa, who is nice as pie and easy on the eye. Melissa's hair, makeup and nails are always immaculate. Melissa wears the latest fashion labels, which wouldn't leave much to your imagination.

They have three spoiled but adorable children who seem to get anything they want. Brad, who I am particularly fond of, is the eldest at eighteen years old. Brad is your typical overconfident brash American teenager, but he could not look more Irish with his red hair and freckled face. His friends call him Flash. In fact, we all call him Flash, because he has flash red hair and everything he does is flash. Like his mother, he has all the latest trends, bling watch, phone, sunglasses. You just have to love Brad.

Brad's sisters, Scarlett and Britney, are sixteen. They are twins! Identical twins, in fact. The three siblings might as well be triplets, with the big flash heads of curly red hair and freckles on them all.

Catherine and her crew arrive first; She is all smiles when we see her. That home sweet home feeling, but it's bittersweet. Catherine suddenly bursts out in tears of emotion when she sees me and Jane. She was so looking forward to getting home. Now the reality of why she has come home has hit her. Our dear Mother would have always been there to greet them at arrivals.

Kisses and hugs all round, the usual, "you've got so tall!" And "have you lost weight?" Great to have them home. We catch up while waiting for Martin's crew. We'll hear them before we see them.

Sure enough, Martin and his crew burst through arrivals as if they were scoring a touchdown at the Super Bowl. High fives and slam dunks all round. That's everyone home and great to see them all looking so well. It's just great to have my family home.

Maurice, Larry, and Curly have scrubbed up well and are on starters orders with the BMW cars. At first I thought maybe they had even matured somewhat. Wishful thinking on my part. They couldn't be more helpful herding everyone into the cars and literally chucking their luggage in the boot. Boys will be boys and once a boy racer, always a boy racer.

I should have known better than giving three competitive lads a BMW each; for the three lads it was, in their minds, a race to the hotel. By the time I arrived at the hotel in my humble taxi, my family had already booked in and were back downstairs in the hotel bar. Poor Cathy needed a brandy. She wasn't a keen flier and was so relieved to have the flight from New York behind her. Cathy said the car journey to the hotel was worse than any flight she had ever experienced.

Having lost our mother to Covid; We, as in, me, Catherine, and Martin, all got letters from an anonymous donor saying, 'an angel was looking over us.' We were all included as joint owners of the Remembrance Gardens at the Grand Hotel

The fact there were so many shareholders didn't matter to our Martin. Or the fact that it was the gardens. He got great joy telling anyone he met at the hotel that he was one of the hotel owners. The gesture seemed to go over his head.

Catherine, on the other hand, thought it was an amazing gesture in memory of all the victims, including our Mother. Catherine and Cathy even went to see where the remembrance garden was to be built. They'll all find out soon enough that it's all in our Mother's name. I so wanted to tell them, but I held myself back. Just wait for a little while longer. The cooling off period was coming to an end. This weekend was the right time to tell Claire and my family.

The young folk got out and about in the city with the three chauffeurs bringing them around. I had a quiet word in their 'shell like.' I told them to slow down and calm down. Jane was in charge and Jane knew Bruce.

The older folk settled down at the bar to catch up. Claire joined us for this. It took about five seconds for Catherine to notice that Claire wasn't drinking alcohol. And so, our good news was out. What about the wedding? We hadn't booked it yet. Martin figured, as one of the hotel owners, he could get us a reduced rate at The Grand Hotel…. at his hotel!

I owned the hotel. Claire and I had already made enquiries. I may well be the hotel owner; I wasn't going to cancel someone else's wedding. The Grand Hotel was booked out for the foreseeable future. This didn't stop alleged hotel owner Martin arguing with the hotel manager. He was disgusted; the best he could do was to get us on a cancellation list.

The conversation didn't take long to get around to the fact that the winning Billion Euro mega jackpot was won in Ireland. It was big news in America, too. When Martin heard that Jack Potter, the Billion Euro winner, was also staying in The Grand Hotel, or his hotel as he liked to put it, he was delighted. "Awesome. Just wait till I tell my buddies back home."

This wasn't exactly 'awesome' for me, it made me feel uneasy. It was a big hotel, but it would only be a matter of time before Martin would bump into Jack Potter. I knew that if this happened, there was a good chance of me getting a bit too close for comfort with Jack Potter.

Next morning there happened to be a chance meeting at the hotel beauty spa. The fiancée of the alleged Billion Euro mega jackpot winner got talking to the wife of one of the alleged hotel owners while they were getting their nails manicured. Peggy Potter bluntly asked Melissa where she bought her lovely 'glad rags.' Melissa, delighted with the compliment, was impressed with Peggy's diamond encrusted necklace, matching bracelet, and massive engagement ring.

That day we all celebrated Angela MacMann's life with a family mass, and lunch. The occasion was both sorrowful and joyful. Everyone cried, everyone laughed. We arranged to have drinks and dinner at The Grand Hotel that evening. I thought to myself that maybe this family gathering would be a good time to tell Claire, and my family, about the real winner of the Billion Euro jackpot.

My plans quickly changed when Claire and I arrived at the hotel that evening. New acquaintances, Melissa and

Peggy, had already introduced their husbands to one another. Not even that. They were all drinking cocktails in the hotel lounge and had been joined by Catherine, Cathy, Zoe, and Ciaran. A few of Jack's pals were there, too.

I was wearing my Mackintosh overcoat. I quickly took it off and hung it by the door as we entered the lounge area. I didn't want to take any chances. As we joined them, I did my best to keep a safe distance between myself and Jack Potter.

Martin did the honours and introduced us to his new best friends, Jack, and Peggy Potter. I did my best to keep a low profile while in their company. This wasn't too hard, as Martin dominated the conversation. He had great ideas about how the Potters could invest their Billion Euro.

Melissa, I noticed, was not her usual smiley self. In fact, she looked embarrassed. Coincidently, Melissa and Peggy were both wearing the same 'glad rags.' The dress, or dresses, left little to the imagination and I have to say, this was unfortunate in Peggy's case. Because of this, Melissa was distancing herself from same-dress-Peggy. I mean, what if someone were to take a photograph!

This affected the seating arrangements. Catherine and Cathy found themselves next to Peggy Potter. Cathy, I should add, worked as a secretary to a lawyer back in New York. They say a little knowledge is a dangerous thing. Cathy and Peggy had a dangerous conversation. Cathy, who wouldn't be accustomed to drinking cocktails, and probably still under the influence of the wine she had at lunch, was intrigued as to why Peggy was marrying Jack again so soon after their divorce.

"Was it because of the Billion Euro he had won?" She suggested. Peggy took offence to this remark. I was worried that things might kick off. Peggy looked like she was fit to burst Cathy.

Cathy, not meaning to cause offence, having 'little knowledge' of events, and worried about the look she was getting from Peggy, then tried to explain, save face, or save her face even! "Peggy, if you and Jack got divorced in January, and the Mega Millions Lottery was won at the end of December, then surely you are entitled to half of the Billion Euro." Cathy's explanation quickly gained offended Peggy Potter's full attention.

"Go on." She said, all ears now but still looking like she was fit to burst someone. A nervous Cathy then explained,

"Peggy, if you and Jack were in fact still married on the thirty-first of December, the day that the lottery draw took place, then surely you are entitled to half of the Billion Euro. You were still Jack's wife when he won the money."

I watched nervously as this revelation began to sink in with Peggy. She looked across the table at Jack Potter with gritted teeth; she looked like she was going to burst him now.

How had she missed this? Was she entitled to half a Billion Euro from her divorce settlement? She didn't need to marry Jack again.

Peggy made excuses and disappeared shortly after this conversation with Cathy. We had Jack and a couple of his cronies' company for another half an hour or so. As we said our goodbyes, I could sense Jack Potter staring at me. He had a quizzical expression. I did my best to avoid eye contact with him.

Still staring at me, Jack suddenly clicked his fingers and pointed at me. "I've met you before, Pal. Where do I know you from?" It caught me unawares, and I just looked at him, startled. There was an uncomfortable silence. Everyone was staring at me now. It was Claire who came to my rescue.

"Mr Potter." Claire's voice drew Jack's gaze away from me. She continued. "We have met you before, at The Crock Of Gold pub. You kindly paid for our lunch that day." This answer seemed to satisfy Jack.

"The name's Jackpot, call me Jackpot." he said to Claire triumphantly as he raised his glass in a cheers motion to all of us. "Call me Jackpot!"

The youngsters all joined us for dinner and a lovely family evening. Twins Scarlett and Britney were wearing the latest silly Jack Potter tee shirts now, along with Jane, of course. They were not impressed, having missed out on meeting Jack Potter. The events with Jack put me off telling the family about the Billion Euro. I just couldn't do it with Jack Potter being in the vicinity.

I noticed Peggy Potter at the reception area with some luggage. It looked like she was checking out of the hotel. She was being helped by her two brothers, Damo and Vince; Damo, I now know, is the Terminator guy who was chasing Jack Potter that day I went to the Lottery head office.

Me, Claire, and Jane met the family for breakfast next morning. Martin was waiting for us at the hotel reception with the hotel manager. They had great news for us. Turned out there was a wedding cancellation after all. "Guess what?" Martin exclaimed excitedly. "You two lovebirds are top of the cancellation list."

The date available was March twenty-seventh. The date we had hoped for. It was almost a year to the day since our own cancelled wedding. Claire was delighted. We both were. Not even that. It was the same hotel where my parents had celebrated their wedding. Claire was also concerned.

"Are you sure we can afford it, Billy? The Grand Hotel!" I put her at ease, told her 'we would manage.' I still had planned on telling Claire and family all about the Billion Euro before the Americans went back.

Jack Potter was also having breakfast. Peggy Potter was not there. Martin went over to say hello. He was hoping to introduce twins Scarlett and Britney to him, maybe get a photo. Martin was told in no uncertain terms to get lost.

Martin didn't react. He let this incident go.

"Nobody is going to take our sunshine away today. We are celebrating." Martin ordered a bottle of champagne with the breakfast to celebrate our good fortune on getting the wedding reception booked. He was going to be my Best Man at the wedding after all.

Chapter 13

I got two significant news bulletins today, well, three news bulletins. The third was not as significant, more interesting really. The first significant news bulletin was from my 'eyes and ears' on the street. They asked me if I knew how Jack Potter got his nickname. I thought it was obvious. Jack Potter to being called Jackpot, had an obvious ring to it. The lads explained that there was another reason he was known as Jackpot. Jack Potter was a gambler.

My eyes and ears on the street informed me that Jack Potter was gambling massive amounts of money. He bet big and occasionally won big. But more often he lost big. Like most gamblers, if he lost, he would bet bigger again to recoup his losses. The word from my eyes and ears on the street was that Jackpot was getting himself into trouble. He had massive gambling debts.

Later that day, I got my second significant news bulletin. This time it was on the news and social media. Peggy Potter had arranged a press conference. Peggy was front and centre. She had her brothers Damien and Vincent on one side and well-known solicitor Percival Higgins on her other side. Jack Potter was not there.

Peggy then made an announcement. Peggy Potter was taking Billion Euro winner Jack Potter to court. She was demanding her half share of the Billion Euro lottery jackpot. Percival Higgins stepped forward and announced they would answer no questions. "Margaret Peggy Potter would have her day in court and her say in court." This was pure gold. Jack Potter just kept on giving as far as news and social media were concerned. The Billion Euro jackpot winner was hot news again: red hot news all around the world.

The third, and only interesting news bulletin, I got from my nephew Brad, or Flash, as he likes to be called. "Have you bought a ticket, Uncle Billy?" he said to me.

"A ticket?" I enquired. "A ticket for what?" Brad was swaggering around the room. He was impersonating Jack Potter now and doing a great impersonation, too.

"Jackpot!" He shouted while waving his arms in the air triumphantly. "The name's Flashpot. Call me Flashpot!"

Brad had a ticket, in fact, he had a handful of tickets. He was flashing them around, showing them off. He had tickets for the new Mega Millions lottery draw. He could not believe I hadn't heard about it and was disappointed with my lack of enthusiasm about it all. "There is a new Billion Bucks up for grabs," he told me excitedly. "Jackpot and his Billion Bucks is old news now, Uncle Billy." There was a new Mega Lottery taking place in April.

As I said, it was just interesting news for me. Maybe there would be a new winner of one Billion Euro, and this would at the very least take the heat off the present Billion Euro winner, make him, or me, old news as Flash had said. Did I buy a ticket? No, not this time, or not yet! I was finding it difficult enough trying to spend the Billion Euro I already had!

It didn't take reporters, including Sandra, long to arrive at The Grand Hotel after Peggy's big announcement. They wanted Jack Potter's opinion on the latest developments with Peggy. And here we were again! Mirroring the day that I first met Jack at Lottery head office.

As it happened, Claire and I had a meeting with the hotel manager to discuss and confirm our wedding reception. When we arrived at the hotel, I had already noticed that Peggy's brother Damo, or Terminator guy as I know him, was hanging around outside in the hotel car park.

I was in the hotel reception area with Claire and the hotel manager. Jack Potter arrived outside the front door, he was immediately surrounded by reporters and photographers. Terminator guy Damo, in the car park, was looking on.

Sandra caught Jack's attention. "Jackpot, are you going to give Peggy her half share of the Billion Euro?" Jack was waving his arms around angrily. He was talking to Sandra but making sure Damo could hear.

"She's not getting another fucking penny. None of them are. Tell them all to go fuck themselves. They won't get a penny more out of me. Put that in your rag of a newspaper for them to see."

Jackpot's friend Macker then got involved. He brought Jack into the hotel and kept the door closed so the reporters couldn't get in. Jack Potter was raging now. His face was red with rage, he was swinging his arms around aimlessly; everyone around reception was keeping a safe distance from him, even his own friends.

Macker tried to talk to him. "Calm down, Jackpot," he said cautiously. And with that, Jack turned around and swung a punch at Macker. He missed. It was a fresh air shot and Jackpot ended up falling on the floor in a heap. It wasn't a pretty sight.

The doors were closed, but the reporters and photographers could see everything that was happening through the windows. Macker, not a bit fazed by events, helped Jackpot to his feet. Jackpot dusted himself down. He looked wildly around the reception area and the mayhem he was causing. His eyes stopped on me and Claire for a few seconds. I was wearing my Mackintosh overcoat.

Still looking in our direction, Jack shouted, "Fuck this shit!" He then turned his attention to Macker beside him, "Let's get the fuck out of here Macker, we need another drink. Pints are on me." With that, Jackpot, Macker, and a couple more of his cronies marched out the hotel doors. As the doors opened, reporters and photographers stepped aside to make room, and for their own safety. They all then turned to follow Jack, shouting questions, and taking photographs.

I wasn't sure what to make of all this. Everything had been going according to plan until now, or according to my new plan. I was nervous about what might happen. Questions were bound to be asked now. And a court case too? I had a bad feeling about it all.

I looked at Claire; she was shocked with what had happened. She wasn't surprised, though. "What did I tell you, Billy? That Jackpot fellow has brought all of this upon himself. I told you; that man will never have peace. He shouldn't have told anyone that he won that Billion Euro, Billy. He should have stayed anonymous. That's what I would have done, Billy."

Claire was right. I also realised that I couldn't tell anyone about the Billion Euro either. Someone always tells; word always gets out. My main concern was what if Jack Potter tells? Jack doesn't know who I am, though. Or does he? I wasn't sure now. I decided to keep the cooling-off period going a bit longer, or at least till this new Jack and Peggy Potter scandal blows over.

It didn't look like this story would blow over in a hurry, though. All of this dominated the news and social media. Front-page headlines in all the newspapers, and not just in Ireland. Jack Potter was world news again. This story was almost as big, if not bigger, than when Jack Potter claimed he won the Billion Euro.

My Americans were hanging around for a few more days. Martin thought the Potter's business was a blast. Jack Potter was still staying in the hotel, Martin's hotel, in his mind. Martin saw Jack at the hotel reception area; he had twins Scarlett and Britney with him. The twins were wearing their silly Jackpot tee shirts, and Martin was hoping to get them both in a photo with Billion Euro Jackpot winner, Jack Potter.

It did not go well. As soon as Martin approached Jack, he was told again, and in no uncertain terms, to get lost. Not even that, Jack Potter, with his crew of hangers on around him, told Martin to keep his family out of Jack's way or there would be trouble. Martin wanted Jack to be kicked out of the hotel.

Martin told us all about this incident at lunch. He just couldn't understand it. He thought they were friends; he had given Jack advice. Melissa had even advised Peggy Potter on where to buy her clothes. I just told him that Jack was erratic and under a lot of stress. Cathy kept her head down, sipped her glass of wine, and said nothing.

The court case was on Friday, which was the same day the Americans were going home. Twins Scarlett and Britney never did get their photograph taken with Jack Potter. They had the latest tee shirts, though, as did Jane. Peggy Potter's face was plastered on some of the tee shirts now. Jane's tee shirt had a slogan saying, 'Free Jack Potter'

I had my own interests to worry about with the court case. I have to say; I was worried about what might happen. There was no way of avoiding this story. It was all over the news and all anyone wanted to talk about. I knew Jack Potter didn't win the Billion Euro jackpot. A few people at Lottery head office knew. I didn't know if Jack Potter had told anyone. I figured that if he hadn't told Peggy; the chances are he hadn't told anyone.

If the true story came out, I figured the Lottery had to keep my name out of this. I had told them I wanted to stay anonymous along with the other family names, which I put down as part of the syndicate. I hadn't given my family their share yet, but that didn't matter for now. My name and their names would have to be kept anonymous. Jack Potter was the only person who went public. I wasn't entirely sure that Jack didn't know who I was. Had he figured it out? I just didn't know for sure after recent events.

I reassured myself that the worst-case scenario would be that Jack would tell what happened. I wouldn't blame him. In fact, Jack has to tell the court what happened because he hasn't got half a Billion Euro to give Peggy if she wins the court case.

If Jack has to give Peggy half his five million Euro, he's still a wealthy man, unless he's gambled it all away. That is Jack and Peggy's business, and nothing to do with me. I gave Jack Potter five million Euro for our arrangement. Five million Euro wasted, you might say. That's not the way I look at it. Things happened for a reason. If I hadn't met Jack Potter and hatched my plan, then I wouldn't have met Austin Goodman later that same day.

The work I had achieved with Austin's help far and away exceeded the five million Euro in my mind. I would call it another positive kick back. Austin's work alone was invaluable and his skills at negotiating the various property deals saved me much more than the five million Euro I had given to Jack Potter.

Friday, the day of the Potter versus Potter court case. I was on airport duty. We were all back on duty; Maurice, Curly, and Larry helped again. I drove to the Airport with Catherine and Cathy in my taxi. There was no way Cathy was getting back in the BMWs with any of the three lads. The three lads brought the rest of the American crew, and Jane, of course.

Everyone was coming back to Dublin in March for the wedding, but the goodbyes at the airport were still hard. We had celebrated our Mother's life. When I say the goodbyes were hard, I mean particularly for me, Catherine, and Martin. The reality struck us, and tears flowed.

Martin's hard shell cracked. He was inconsolable. Our Mother would have always been there to see the Americans off and his emotions let flow. Catherine, Martin, and I had a group hug. Martin, barely able to talk with emotion, just whispered, "See you in March little Bro, let us know when that memorial garden is finished."

Emotions back in check, the phones were out and lots of photos taken to be cherished and posted on social media. As we got the traditional family selfie, I found myself between the twins, Scarlett, and Britney. As the cameras were snapping, the twins told me they had a fantastic time in Ireland. Their only regret was that they never got a photo with the Irish winner of the Billion Euro Jackpot, to show their friends back home. I just smiled, put my arms around them and said, "Look at the cameras, girls; Say cheese."

As my family departed, I regretted not telling them about the lottery win. I hadn't even given them any of their share yet. It would have to wait a little longer. They were all doing well in America. With me buying the family home, Catherine and Martin had also received their share of our mother's estate. I didn't tell them I bought it, not yet anyways.

I figured I would wait and see how Jack and Peggy Potter's court case fared out first. Let it blow over, let the dust settle and then tell them. I'm sure that's what Claire would advise, too. A bit of another 'cooling-off period,' as she puts it.

Chapter 14

The 'Potter versus Potter' court case was broadcast live on television and social media. I was glued to proceedings. As things happened, like Jack and Peggy's rekindling, it turned out to be a short affair. In fact, it was all over in less than an hour, not the drawn-out saga that reporters had hoped for.

Jack Potter was representing himself. Peggy's solicitor, Percival Higgins, opened proceedings with a well-prepared speech on how his poor client, Margaret Peggy Potter, had been deceived by her Billionaire ex-husband. He even suggested that Jack Potter should go to jail for attempting to steal his client's rightful half share of one Billion Euro. Percival was constantly interrupted by Jack Potter.

The date of their marriage was mentioned, the terms of their divorce, the date of the lottery draw and, crucially, the date of their divorce. Jack and Peggy Potter were divorced after the lottery was won.

Jack Potter had one witness in court: Edward Davenport. He was there in all his pomp. I had phoned Mr Davenport to get his advice. I wanted to ensure that my name remained anonymous during the court case. It was Edward who suggested he could be a witness for Jack Potter in court. It was being broadcast live on television and social media, after all.

The Judge and Jack Potter were not strangers. With Jacks shady history, It wasn't the first time they had met in court. Jack wouldn't stop talking and interrupting proceedings, so the judge threw him out for contempt of court. The judge then called on Mr Edward Davenport to speak.

Edward Davenport confirmed the fact that Jack Potter was a winner of the Billion Euro, but only as part of a syndicate. Edward showed the judge a photocopy of Jack Potter's cheque, the amount he received from the total jackpot; The cheque was for five million Euro.

Edward pointed out that the other winners had a legal right to remain Anonymous. He confirmed that a person who must remain anonymous added Mr Jack Potter to the syndicate. This happened on January the seventh. Crucially, this was one week after the official divorce date of Jack and Margaret Peggy Potter.

The judge ruled that Mr Davenport's evidence was all that mattered. Mr Jack Potter did not have to give any money to his ex-wife, Margaret Peggy Potter. The fact that Jack had probably squandered most of his money wasn't mentioned and was irrelevant.

Jack Potter celebrated as if he had, in fact, won the Billion Euro. "Jackpot!" he shouted from the back of the court where he had managed to sneak back in. Peggy was ashen faced. She looked like she was about to burst. She stormed out of the court with her two brothers and solicitor trailing behind.

There was a big question left unanswered now. If Jack Potter got five million Euro, who was the real Mega Millions Jackpot winner? Who got the other nine hundred and ninety-five million Euro? No doubt the media will ask this question now. No doubt Sandra Birch will have something to say about all of this.

I wasn't too worried about events at this stage. Edward Davenport had said in court that lottery jackpot winners had a right to stay anonymous, and the judge agreed. That was all I wanted from the start. I go back to my original plan so; I keep the head down, keep the good work going, then tell

Claire and family when this story blows over, or after the new cooling-off period.

I met Jane unexpectedly. It was raining, so Jane phoned me to see if I could pick her up in town and bring her home. Her mother and Michael were working on a big story for the next day's paper and were too busy. I was just delighted to see her. She was drenched from the rain when I collected her. She was wearing skimpy shorts and another one of her tee shirts, no coat to cramp her style. So, I threw my overcoat over her and got her into the car. The battery on her phone was almost dead, which was good for me because I got some chat from her.

Except for being soaked, Jane was in great form. She had seen Bruce and The Duke in town; they had both been delighted to see her, and The Duke was back to himself again. She'd had a blast with her American cousins and was chuffed because Claire had asked her to be a bridesmaid at our wedding in March. As we got near the end of our journey, Jane asked me if I had heard the latest about her massive TikTok following. "TikTok?" I said. "I don't do TikTok Jane. Does your mum know about this TikTok?"

"Mum's on TikTok! Everyone is on TikTok, Dad!" Was her answer, making me feel old and not with the times.

"I'll check it out Jane; did you send me that TikTok friend request yet?" Jane just looked at me with her teenage stare.

"Ye… sure thing, Dad."

I couldn't resist probing Jane out for information.

"So…. you say your Mother and Michael are working on a big story then. No doubt about the real Billion Euro lottery winner…. I suppose." Jane was on her phone now, trying to squeeze the last few seconds left on her battery.

"Ye, she's busy with that story Dad, she's like a woman possessed, I just try to stay out of her way, you know what she's like!"

"Ah, okay, I wouldn't blame you for staying out of the way, Jane. Has she any idea who the real Billion Euro winner is?" Jane put her phone in her pocket; the battery had finally given up.

"Mum's obsessed with a photograph that Michael took. I'd show you only my phone has died. This is massive, Dad. Bigger than anything that has happened so far." We arrived at Jane's house. "It will be in the newspapers tomorrow, Dad. You'll see the photo then. I gotta go. I'm busy too, I'm making a new TikTok video. Thanks for the lift."

As Jane got out of the car, she went to hand back my overcoat, but paused for a few seconds. Jane was staring at the overcoat. "This is perfect, Dad! It's just what I need; Can I borrow it?" I didn't know what she meant. I mean, it was raining, but why would Jane want to borrow my overcoat? I thought maybe she meant borrow it to keep her dry when she went from the car to the front door. Before I had a chance to answer.

"Thanks Dad, I'll give it back to you tomorrow, or the next day. Love you!" She ran into the house with my overcoat tucked under her arm, as if she was trying to keep it dry from the rain.

"Love you too." I shouted after her. The front door was opened, in she went without looking back, and the door slammed shut behind her.

I did think it was odd that Jane borrowed my overcoat. I didn't know what Jane knew; the big story that was going to hit the news next day. Sandra had a big story coming out, a story centred on a certain photograph of a mysterious man with a Mackintosh overcoat.

Chapter 15

Next day Sandra's story was in the newspaper. I had no idea what was about to happen, or what was happening already. I didn't see or hear about Sandra's story until the afternoon. By then, things had really taken off, or kicked off even.

Sandra's story got picked up by other news agencies around the world. On top of this, maybe even to top it all; Jane made a new TikTok video for her thousands of followers. The video was already going viral. She had posted her video the night before, and twelve hours is an eternity on TikTok.

Claire had a busy day and left the house before me. She was meeting her sister, Emily. They were looking at wedding dresses, bridesmaid dresses and other wedding stuff, I suppose. Bridesmaid Jane was tagging along too at some point.

"Have a great time," I told Claire as I waved her off. She was so excited.

"You too," she said, and "don't wait up," she joked. What a day I was about to have, though.

I had a busy day myself. I was giving away one of the new cars, so I had to see a man about a dog. Or more precisely, a man about dogs. After that I had a meeting at The Grand Hotel to discuss the memorial garden and I also had a meeting with Austin pencilled in.

When Catherine was home, she saw on the news someone she'd been to school with. He was being celebrated for his great work training guide dogs for the blind and visually impaired. He was a volunteer and did all this in his own time. I decided to give this man a new BMW.

Maurice was delivering the car. He delivered the car with a simple message from an anonymous donor. 'Thank you.' All this time I was unaware that Sandra's story was already on news sites all around the world and Jane's video had already been viewed by millions on TikTok.

My meeting at The Grand Hotel went well. I gave the go ahead for work on the garden of remembrance. I'd had a great morning, so I was in good form heading to Austin's office for our meeting. I was early, so I had time to grab a coffee in a shop before our meeting. I was intrigued as to what the newspapers had to say, really. Hadn't Jane told me Sandra and Michael had a big story. I imagined there would be a photo of Jack Potter in all the newspapers, no doubt celebrating his victory in court.

As I waited for my coffee, I peeked at the newspaper headlines. I saw the photograph immediately; The photograph was in all the newspapers. It was the same photograph which spooked me the day after I collected the winnings, the one that had me in the background. It was tucked away on page four then. Now it was on the front page. Not even that, it was an enlarged version, pretty much the whole front page.

It was a photograph of Sandra, microphone in hand, talking to Jack Potter when he walked out of Lottery head office claiming to have won the Billion Euro. The emphasis of the photograph this time was the figure in the background, behind Sandra and Jack Potter. The newspaper headlines asked the question; 'Who Is The Man With The Mackintosh Overcoat?' It was me. I was on the front page of all the newspapers.

It seemed to take an age for my coffee cup to fill as I stared at all the newspaper headlines in shock. I grabbed a newspaper and went to pay, while looking around, in case anyone would recognise me. I thought maybe the cashier might recognise me, so I put the newspaper on the counter with the photograph facing down. I was relieved that Jane had borrowed my overcoat because I wasn't wearing it now as a result.

I got back in my car. My hand was shaking as I sipped my coffee. 'Okay Billy, calm yourself down,' I told myself. I knew it was me in the photograph. I reassured myself with the fact that Sandra and Michael had done the story; they hadn't recognised me so realistically nobody else would.

There was much more to Sandra's story. Sandra reported on the various good deeds happening around the city and beyond. Sandra hinted that if she got the answer to her first question, as in, 'Who was the man with the Mackintosh overcoat?' Then she may well have the answer to the other question; 'Who is the real winner of the Billion Euro Jackpot?'

My immediate thought was that I had to phone Claire. We were way past cooling-off periods and waiting for dust to settle. I should have told Claire from the start, now here I was on the front page of the newspapers. I was sure that Claire would recognise me when she saw it. So, I phoned her. I needed to meet her before she saw the newspapers. I needed to tell Claire everything, and it's not the type of conversation you want to have over the phone. The phone call was bad timing. Claire's phone was answered, but it was her sister Emily on the other end.

I thought it was Claire, naturally enough. I probably sounded a bit frantic. "Claire, where are you? We need to meet." The reply from Emily at the other end was,

"Well, you'll just have to wait, Billy, but believe me when I say, it will be worth it when you see her." There was a couple of seconds' pause while I figured out who I was talking to.

"Emily? Any chance I can talk to Claire for a few seconds?" There was a bit of laughing and giggling in the background, then Emily spoke again.

"Claire is trying on a beautiful wedding dress for you, Billy, so she can't talk right now." Another voice came on the line; it was Jane this time.

"Hi Dad, we're having a blast of a day, and guess what Dad? We've picked out our bridesmaids' dresses." Jane excitedly described the bridesmaid's dresses in minute detail. I was getting vibes that I wouldn't get talking to Claire.

"They sound lovely, Jane; I can't wait to see them…. Any chance I can talk to Claire for a second?" There was muffled talk and whispering. I could hear Emily say it would be bad luck for Billy to talk to Claire when she was wearing her wedding dress. Emily was back on the line.

"Claire wants to know. Is everything okay, Billy? Can she phone you later?" Another pause while I thought of what to say.

"Emily, tell Claire everything is great. I'll phone her back later. I can't wait to see you all in your gorgeous dresses."

I had wanted to tell Claire before I told anyone else but knew realistically I wouldn't see her until later in the day. I needed to tell someone. I needed advice. I had my meeting with Austin and decided I would tell him at the meeting. I figured Austin would give me sensible advice.

I took a deep breath as I got to the front door of Austin's premises. I was about to knock, but Austin's wife, Sinead, opened the door. She just smiled, then led me to Austin's desk without saying a word.

Austin was sitting at his desk. He barely acknowledged my arrival. There was a newspaper in front of him on his desk. He looked up briefly and motioned for me to sit down without saying a word. He was staring at the newspaper, or more precisely, the photograph on the front page. He had a broad smile on his face. I sensed he knew. There was an uncomfortable silence, so I started the conversation.

"Austin, I'm so sorry. I should have been honest with you from the start." Austin put his hand out in a stop motion. I stopped talking. He looked up at me now. The smile was gone; he was more serious, business-like.

"What does Claire think of all this?" he said. It was a question I had been asking myself; what will Claire make of all this?

"I haven't told her yet Austin, I haven't had a chance. Nobody knows; and now.... well now everyone is going to know."

"No, Billy, this is your secret." He paused and then corrected himself. "This can be our secret. You can't tell anyone yet, not even Claire." He had a serious expression on his face. He was thinking. "Jack Potter!" He suddenly said, "Jack Potter was there that day; surely he knows who you are?"

"Nobody knows." I said again. I pointed to the newspaper on his desk. "Well, you know now, and anyone else who recognises me from that photograph." Austin picked up the newspaper and looked at the photograph, then brushed the newspaper aside casually.

"I didn't recognise you in the photograph, Billy; it's a bit blurry really and you have a mask covering half your face. I just kind of figured things out. You were either a drugs lord, a mafia boss, or you won the lottery." He had a chuckle to himself, then continued. "The photograph just confirmed my suspicions. We met that evening, you'll remember. You were wearing the Mackintosh overcoat."

Austin stood up and started walking around his office. He was looking at his framed pictures and comics on his wall. He stopped at one and adjusted it slightly, made sure it was straight and in line with the others. He was in serious thought. Without turning around, he said, "I noticed that you're not wearing the overcoat today, Billy." He turned and faced me now. "You have to keep wearing it, keep things normal, no changes to the routine if you know what I mean, otherwise people will wonder why; they'll think you have something to hide, a secret even."

"I do have something to hide, Austin! I have an incredible secret. Things are getting out of control here, out of my control. All I intended was to help a few people, and no matter what, I wanted to stay anonymous. Now we have this." I pointed to the newspaper again.

"Sandra Birch will be your main concern here, Billy. It's all a bit too close to home for you, with Sandra and Jane in the thick of it all. Sandra has been snooping around town lately, even asking about my business."

Austin sat down at his desk again. He took the newspaper, folded it, and put it in a drawer under his desk. "You've got to get the overcoat back from Jane; you need to do that today." This statement caught me by surprise because I hadn't told Austin that Jane had borrowed it. I paused for breath.

"Austin, all these good things that are happening; I mean, we've done so much Austin, we've both been doing this. I couldn't have done all of this without you. We're in this together, a team even. The thing is Austin, a lot of the stuff in Sandra's story has nothing to do with me, nothing to do with us." The broad smile was back on Austin's face again.

"Billy, can't you see that all of these other things, or stuff, as you put it. All this stuff is happening because of you! That's what makes you so exceptional. You are out there doing these exceptional good deeds for people. Can't you see what's happening beyond this?"

"Austin!" I was protesting now. "I have all this money; all I am doing is helping a few people and thanking a few people who helped me or helped others even." He stood up again.

"That's how they all started Billy, selfless acts." He was pointing to his framed photographs on the wall now. "You're right, a lot of these good deeds are being done by others, but you lit the fuse, Billy. You started this, and it's being copied everywhere now. Giving is contagious Billy, you have given so much, the goodness has spread. You put a couple of doctors and nurses on the streets to help. Now other doctors and nurses have volunteered their time. Before you knew it, cities around the world copied this. The same is happening with the vets, the hostels too Billy. Random people are anonymously paying for hostel beds and meals to help the homeless. You started this, Billy, and it's being copied everywhere."

I hadn't realised all of this was happening. I was thinking of all the things I had done and how I'd liked to get a 'kick back' of some sort whenever I could. Could it really be possible that all these other kick backs were happening because of me?

I thought for a few seconds. Austin was waiting for me to say something, waiting for my reaction.

"Like I said, Austin, I just want to stay anonymous. I don't want all this attention around me, so it ends now. I need to go home and talk to Claire, tell her everything. This will all blow over...." And I could hardly believe I heard myself saying it to Austin.... "This will all blow over after a cooling-off period."

He was slowly nodding his head from side to side now as if to say, no chance, Billy. "It's just a newspaper story, Austin. There will be a new story tomorrow, and this will all be yesterday's news." I said it more in hope than actual belief. Austin stood up now. He took the newspaper back out from his drawer and laid it out on the table in front of me.

"This is just the beginning Billy, its already world news, and then there's Jane's video. What about Jane's TikTok video, and all the copycat videos?" I didn't know what he meant.

"Videos?" I enquired. "What videos?" Austin looked surprised by my question. He went to his office door, opened it, and called Sinead inside to join us. He put his hand gently on her shoulder and whispered something in her ear and said,

"Thank you Sinead." Still holding the door open, he let Sinead out, then came back and sat down opposite me again. He looked me straight in the eyes now. "You really haven't seen Jane's TikTok video, have you?" He smiled now, in disbelief.

"I don't do TikTok, Austin."

There was a knock on the door, and it opened slowly. It was Sinead. Austin gestured for her to come inside. Sinead had an iPad with her. She placed it on the desk in front of me and looked at Austin, who gave a nod of approval. She pressed play, and there it was. Jane's TikTok video, with Jane, and my Mackintosh overcoat.

The video was about twenty seconds long. It was good, a bit of fun even. It was a video with Jane and Sandra. They had kind of recreated the photograph, except it was Jane who had the Mackintosh overcoat trailing behind her, cape like, instead of me. "Okay, I get it Austin. It's harmless enough. Jane was just copying the newspaper story. My overcoat is there alright but there is no mention or reference to me. Seems it's more about Sandra, really." Austin looked at Sinead, who was standing behind me.

"How many views now, Sinead?" Sinead looked over my shoulder at the iPad.

had nearly forty million views so far. It's the number one trending video on TikTok. and not even that, there are hundreds of copycat videos already." Austin was looking at me, looking for my reaction.

"Thank you Sinead, that will be all for now," he said. Sinead left us on our own again. Austin looked across the desk at me, still looking for my reaction, then said, "The video is called, Who is the man with the Mackintosh overcoat? Is it Mack Man?" I couldn't think straight. I didn't know what to make of everything that was happening.

"Forty million, that's hard to believe really, Austin." I finally said. Austin was getting more animated now.

"Forty million so far, Billy! Who knows what or where this will all lead to?" I thought for a few seconds, weighing up events in my head.

"Nothing really changes, Austin. I'm not in the video. I'm sure I'm not mentioned in any of Jane's videos, for that matter."

"Not in the video! Not mentioned!" He exclaimed. Then he almost said it but stopped mid-sentence. "Of course you are mentioned; you are Mack…" He stopped short of finishing the sentence, then quickly changed track. He took a calming breath. "Maybe this will all blow over after a few days, but it's a big maybe, I'm sure of that. You have to be ready all the same, Billy, ready for any awkward questions." He contemplated for a few seconds, then continued. "If I figured it out, then others will do the same. That Sandra Birch, she's no fool, as you know. You have to be on your guard with her."

My phone rang; it was Claire phoning me back. I stared at my phone but didn't answer it. I wasn't ready to talk; I wasn't sure what the conversation would be about. Austin sensed or knew from my reaction that the phone call was from Claire.

"She doesn't need to know, at least not yet. If you want to stay anonymous, then the fewer people who know, the better." The phone rang out unanswered.

"We'll see Austin. I'll phone Claire back when we're done here." I stood up to leave; I needed to get my head around things. "Austin, for all we know, Claire might have been phoning because she saw the newspapers. Maybe she recognised me from the photograph. I wouldn't know what to say to her." I took a deep breath. "It's better that I tell Claire than she finds out by some other means. She deserves that."

I felt I was way in over my head now. It seemed like the more I had done to stay anonymous, the more need arose to stay anonymous. This was getting way too big. Things were getting out of control. We shook hands and agreed to meet in a few days to discuss developments, if any. I still wasn't sure what sort of chat I would have with Claire. There was Jane too, I was worried what effect this might have on Jane. Austin could sense how anxious I was.

"Billy, keep a low profile out there. Carry on as normal for now." I just nodded in agreement with him as I went to leave. "Remember, Billy, the worst thing that can happen is people finding out who you are and what you have done. If you think about it; It's all good Billy. You can be very proud of all the good deeds you are doing out there." I really wasn't sure what to make of the meeting with Austin. I was still so nervous and anxious about being found out, being exposed.

I phoned Claire back as soon as I finished the meeting with Austin. We met for lunch, all four of us; Jane, and Emily, tagged along. They were all so excited. Halfway through their shopping day and lots picked out for the wedding already. Jane fidgeted with her phone for practically the whole time. Checking TikTok and updating her friends.

I told Jane I had seen her video, more to judge her reaction, to see if she even had a hint that the person she had made the video about was in fact me, her Father. Not at all. Jane was just happy that I enjoyed it. "Nearly forty-five million views now, Dad. Can you believe it?" What could I say?

"That's amazing, Jane!" I managed to say. It was amazing after all, even if it didn't do me any favours. It impressed Claire and Emily, too.

"Seems like we have a celebrity in the family," Said Emily, before asking me, "Have you seen the newspaper with the photograph?"

"I think I saw it somewhere, Emily," I said, while trying to gauge if any of them even had an inkling of suspicion. Claire was nodding her head from side to side disapprovingly.

"That man and his family will have no peace if they figure out who he is," she said. "Why can't they back off and leave him alone? If he wants to stay anonymous, let him be."

I didn't tell Claire, I just couldn't. Claire and Jane were just enjoying their day, doing normal things. No fuss or no worries about reporters following them. I thought it best to keep it this way for as long as I could, or at least until I could come up with a plan, a new plan.

Chapter 16

My original plan to just walk into the lottery, claim the jackpot, and walk away anonymously seemed so long ago now. So much had happened since then, but it had all been good. So many people had benefited already. I wondered if I had just stuck to the plan as I stepped off that bus. Where would I be now? The dust would have been well settled and nobody would even be talking about the Billion Euro winner. Granted, it would have been mentioned now and again, but it wouldn't be front page news anymore by a long shot.

Now, here we are, front page news again, everyone still looking for the Billion Euro winner. Not even that, people looking for the so-called 'Man with the Mackintosh overcoat' or 'Mack Man.' A simple photograph has somehow resulted in creating some sort of hero to the people.

Practically everything I have done to stay anonymous has had the opposite effect. I'm one of the richest people in Ireland and I should be just taking it easy in a fancy house and fancy car with my wonderful wife-to-be. I felt like a wanted man, but something else was happening to me.

As nervous as I was about being exposed, there was something else I wondered about myself. Was I enjoying the secrecy surrounding it all? I was anonymous and everybody the world over wanted to know who I was. Who was the man with the Mackintosh overcoat? Who was Mack Man even? I buttoned up my overcoat with pride every time I left the house. I still had so much more I wanted to do. I was a man on a mission.

Not only was I getting positive kick backs; I was getting a kick from the entire buzz surrounding everything. I was determined to give most of the money away from the start and determined to stay anonymous, but I started to wonder. What was my real kick back? Was I getting a kick from being the anonymous man everyone was looking for? Was I enjoying the secrecy, the notoriety of it all?

Another thing was happening, too. As I said, I was giving huge amounts of money away. I was also investing huge amounts. The Grand Hotel, in particular, was a massive outlay. This didn't bother me, though; I still owned the hotel. It was in my parents' memory, and the gardens were in memory of all Covid victims. I was investing in other projects too, with Austin Goodman's advice.

I had bought adjacent land near the hotel at the same time along with other property. It seemed like the more money I spent or gave away, the more I was making at the same time. I had bought shares in a pharmaceutical company that was working on a covid vaccine. I figured I was helping somehow to get the vaccine out to the public. Did I get a kick back? I got a massive kick back; these shares had now skyrocketed in value.

I was giving huge amounts of money away, but I was also investing huge amounts too. I didn't want to be a Billionaire but the more I gave money away; it seemed the more I was getting back on my investments. I could have been exposed as the Billion Euro winner at any moment. That would have been bad enough, but realistically it would have blown over after a so-called cooling-off period. People who knew me would always know, but the rest of the world would have moved on, eventually.

I had a bit of protection in that I had a right to remain anonymous as a lottery winner. Mr Davenport had said this in court, and the judge agreed with him. The questions

Sandra Birch and Jane had now asked; 'Who is the man with the Mackintosh coat?' And 'Who is Mack Man?' This was different. The media storm around this was massive; I had no right to be anonymous if they named me as 'The man with the Mackintosh overcoat,' or 'Mack Man,' I felt more exposed now.

I had done so much with the money, but I was determined to keep it going. There were so many other things happening, too. The good deeds continued to be copied everywhere, but even more so now because of the publicity surrounding Sandra's story and Jane's TikTok video. Kick backs as far as I was concerned. Most of these good deeds were being attributed to Mack Man, whether I was involved or not.

The media had created this Mack Man character, and now it was as if Mack Man was everywhere; and in a roundabout way he was because not only were the good deeds being copied. There were copycat Mack Man's too. People everywhere were now claiming to be Mack Man or pretending to be him, even.

It became a bit of a fad, especially with the followers of Jane's TikTok video. A few of the copycats were chancres. Some were looking for credit or publicity, but most just did it for the fun of it all. Social media was creating a monster, a good monster maybe. It seemed like Mack Man was getting bigger by the day, by the hour even.

Jane's original video was a harmless bit of fun, with the Mackintosh overcoat flaying behind her, looking like a cape. The copycat videos took a different slant on things. In the copycat videos, people were replacing the overcoat with real capes, all kinds of capes.

The mask, which originally was a protection mask I picked up at the lottery office, was an important feature too; I was wearing it in the photo. Jane hadn't worn a mask in her TikTok video. People were wearing masks now in their videos and this was significant, too. It added more mystery to the character. Made it seem more like a masked crusader, or dare I say it, a superhero even.

Things were moving up several notches now, and Sandra found herself in the thick of it all. The same media, who had sought her insight when Jack Potter was in the news, now wanted her expert opinion on 'The man with the Mackintosh overcoat' or 'Mack Man.' It was Sandra's story, after all. This put her back in the spotlight again. Sandra had asked the question. She needed to find the answer now to her own question. The question the entire world was asking. Who is the man with the Mackintosh overcoat? Who is Mack Man?

Maurice, Curly, and Larry told me that Sandra was like a woman possessed rushing around town, following up on every lead, every clue. With the various copycat good deeds and people claiming to be Mack Man, there was so much confusion for her, and this suited me. The more confusion, the better.

I carried on as normal, or as normal as I could really, just like Austin suggested. I even called to collect my overcoat from Jane. I was delighted to be seeing her but wary of bumping into Sandra and Michael. Jane answered the door, big hug, and all. Jane was minding her brother and sister. Bad luck for Jane maybe, but a bit of good luck for me. I knew this meant her mother and Michael were out.

Now, more often than not, I'd be lucky to get more than a few words from Jane and this would have suited just fine this day. I could collect my Mackintosh overcoat and leave before Sandra and Michael got back to make things uncomfortable. Not this day. Jane was in flying form. I got the entire story about her TikTok video. How it was one of the most watched videos 'ever!' In fact, Jane wouldn't shut up. Sure enough, a car pulls into the driveway and sure enough, it was Sandra and Michael.

I stood awkwardly on the front doorstep as Sandra and Michael got out of their car; they were not in a good mood by the looks of them. Sandra and I were generally civil to one another. She was a good mother and had been mostly good at letting me spend time with Jane over the years.

Sandra did come out with more than the odd snide remark over the years, though. I tended to avoid her if I could. This was difficult when Jane was young, but it was easier now. Jane was older and more independent. I had the other reason to avoid Sandra now.

I always got the impression that Sandra looked down on me. She was a bit of a snob, even. I learnt the hard way not to react to any of her smart comments because, as a single father; it was a bad idea to get into an argument with your child's mother. It tends to cost you precious time with your child. I got in the habit of letting things go, holding my tongue.

I particularly remember one time. I was dropping Jane home and Sandra answered the door. Sandra had obviously had a glass or two of wine. Jane had received a less than favourable report from school that day. As I walked away, Sandra remarked, "Jane, if you don't work harder in school, you'll end up driving a taxi like your Father."

There were other snide comments over the years too, plenty of them. I learnt to let them go, take a deep breath, count to ten, avoid an argument. Jane was older now and able to make her own decisions. I still tended to let things go most of the time.

Sandra and Michael were talking as they got out of the car. It was obvious what they were talking about; the same thing everyone else was talking about, their big news story, or me, I suppose. They continued talking or arguing, really, almost oblivious to the fact that I was standing on the doorstep with Jane. Tensions were high between them. I could tell they were under pressure from their tone. Sandra had slammed her car door shut and barked at Michael, "Why haven't we found this man? Someone out there must know who he is."

Jane knew why I had called; my overcoat, but she was so excited and talking so much that she had forgotten. Sandra was getting her things from the boot of the car. I told Jane that I had to go. I lied that I had a taxi collection at the airport, and that I was running late. I didn't dare ask Jane for my overcoat, not with Sandra and Michael so close. Oblivious to the fact that her Mother and Michael were talking, an excited Jane burst out with, "Mum, Mum, you won't believe it, more than fifty million views of my video now on TikTok. Can you believe it? Fifty Million views!"

"That's great." Sandra said, dismissively. I could tell that Sandra was feeling the pressure. Everyone wanted to read and hear Sandra's story now. Various news and media outlets around the world had interviewed her. I knew that if that wasn't enough pressure for Sandra to deal with; she was under more and more pressure to come up with the answer to her question. The pressure was getting to her now and she couldn't hide it.

I gave Jane a quick kiss and a hug. Told her I would phone her later and made my escape before Sandra and Michael made it to the front door. "Good to see you, Sandra, and you, Michael." I said as I passed them on the driveway. Sandra mumbled something inaudible under her breath. Michael replied,

"Good to see you too, Billy." I was away to my car with no major incidents. Or so I thought.

"Wait, Dad! Wait there." Jane, shouting from the door, and over her Mother and Michael, had my attention, had everyone's attention. Before I could even acknowledge her, Jane was already on her way back into the house. Sandra and Michael stood in the driveway, waiting. I knew what was coming; I was powerless to do anything. Jane was back out of the house almost as quick as she'd gone in, but she had my overcoat with her now.

"Dad, you forgot your Mackintosh overcoat," she shouted from the front door, and over Sandra and Michael's heads again.

I stood motionless beside my car. I thought that now I'd have to walk back past Sandra and Michael, get the overcoat and then walk back past them again, but with the now famous Mackintosh overcoat in my hand. I needn't have worried. Jane threw the overcoat over her shoulder and, mimicking her own TikTok video, she ran down the driveway past her Mother and Michael towards me. The overcoat flayed cape like behind her, with Jane shouting,

"Is it a bird? Is it a plane? No! It's Mack Man." I burst out laughing.

"Brilliant Jane." Michael found it funny and tried to stifle his laugh when he noticed the sour look on Sandra's face. She didn't look impressed. Jane handed me the overcoat. "Thanks Jane, I'll phone you later."

Sandra and Michael were still in the driveway, still looking stressed, particularly Sandra, by the look on her face. If only they knew how close the person they were looking for was.

Now, I could have just thrown the overcoat in the back of my car and driven off into the sunset. I'm not sure what I was thinking. I was revelling in my secret now. I put my overcoat on and buttoned it up. I took my time; I was teasing them now. Sandra stopped talking or stopped giving Michael a hard time. She watched as I fastened each button.

She turned to face Michael, and in a voice loud enough so that I would hear, said; "Look Michael, he thinks he's Mack Man." They both laughed at this remark. 'Count to ten, Billy, let it go Billy,' I told myself, but I couldn't resist it. As I got in my car to leave, I said,

"Oh, but I am Mack Man, Sandra. I've always been Mack Man; I'm Billy MacMann. Have a nice day, you two."

Chapter 17

As much as I enjoyed teasing Sandra and Michael, Austin was right. Everything was a bit too close to home, with Jane doing the TikTok video and Sandra hot on my tail. It was just a matter of time before I was going to be exposed, found out.

I wasn't doing anything wrong; on the contrary, it was all good that I was doing. This Mack Man character wasn't real, it was a fragment of social media. I didn't see myself as Mack Man or The Man With The Mackintosh Overcoat, this was all nonsense, a bit of fun, like Jane's TikTok video.

My attitude was changing, though. I wore my overcoat with pride; it felt like a symbol of the good work I was doing. I always wore a face mask. A lot of people were still wearing them, so it was no big deal. The mask helped give me a sense of being anonymous.

There were plenty of people wearing Mackintosh overcoats. There always was. They just seemed more noticeable now, and we had the copycats out there having a bit of fun too. You got the odd joker on the street. 'Hey look, it's Mack Man.' I just laughed it off and gave them the same answer I gave Sandra. 'Yes, I'm Mack Man, I'm Billy MacMann.' I didn't deny it, so nobody suspected. It was the perfect cover, really; I was just another Mack Man copycat as far as anyone was concerned, or just a man with a Mackintosh overcoat.

I had spent so much energy trying to stay anonymous, but more often, my actions had only resulted in other reasons to stay anonymous. So, I stopped trying. I had a different mindset now. If I get found out, I get found out. What will be will be. It was working too. Nobody suspected who I was. I was still anonymous.

Claire was busy organising things for our wedding, and the new baby. It was about three weeks before the wedding now. My family would be home again in about two weeks. I figured if I had kept my secret this long, then another couple of weeks wouldn't make much difference. I would tell Claire and my family before the wedding.

The taxi was a brilliant cover for me. I felt guilty not being truthful with Claire. She thought I was out working in my taxi every day. I was working, just not as a taxi driver. I was doing great work out there. I wasn't doing anything wrong, and besides, I had tried to tell Claire about the Billion Euro. It was Claire who talked me out of it. The cooling-off period was all her idea.

It just seemed that every time I tried to end the cooling-off period, something new heated things up again.

First, we had Jack Potter staying in the same hotel as my family. Then we had the realisation that the real winner was still out there and now we had this so-called 'Mack Man' or 'man with a Mackintosh overcoat' nonsense. I needed things to cool down again.

Did Claire notice anything different? Or anything different about me, even? We had a conversation. Claire had said to me, "There is something different about you, Billy; I can't put my finger on it, but something different." I thought maybe she suspected.

"What do you mean, different? Do you mean in a good way or a bad way?" Truth is, it was all good. We were getting on better than ever. We had a wedding and a new baby to look forward to and on top of that; I still had to tell her about the lottery win.

I had another meeting with Austin. He was the only person I could confide in. I hoped for a bit of common sense, a bit of clarity. Surely Austin would agree with me that this Mack Man nonsense would all blow over after a short while. Things would cool down. Austin was level-headed, and I thought he might put me at ease. I couldn't have been more wrong.

Sinead let me in and directed me towards Austin's office. I sat opposite him at his desk. He didn't even look up to acknowledge me. He was busy working on something on the desk. He continued with his work, and still not looking up, casually said. "I see you're wearing the Mackintosh overcoat again. That's a good idea." I was about to answer him when I looked and realised what he was so busy working on.

It was upside down from my viewpoint, but Austin had a copy of the same photograph that was in all the newspapers. The photograph of me, or 'the man with the Mackintosh overcoat.' The photograph that had sparked all this nonsense off. He also had a photo frame; he was carefully placing the photo in the frame. Meticulously, making sure it was straight.

I was a bit taken aback; I didn't know what to say. Austin said nothing; he just continued with his task at hand.

"Is that what I think it is, Austin?" I finally said. He didn't answer me. Happy with his work, he stood up with the now framed photograph. He then turned to the wall behind him. There was already a space made amongst his collection of photos and memorabilia. He carefully hung the framed photograph, stood back to check it, adjusted it slightly on the wall. He then casually sat back down at his desk again.

Remarkably, and as if nothing had happened, he then looked at me and casually said,

"Sorry about that, Billy. Now, what can I do for you today?" I thought maybe he was joking, just having a bit of fun with me. I didn't know Austin long, but from what I knew of him, I would say he was a serious character, not inclined to do jokes or pranks.

There was an awkward silence as we both sat there; at least it was awkward for me. Austin looked comfortable enough, smug even. I didn't know what to say, so I decided to say nothing and see where Austin went with this. He just sat there with a big smile on his face. This was a different Austin Goodman than the one I thought I knew. The serious professional demeanour was gone. He was like an excited child now; He could barely contain himself.

He realised I wasn't going to say anything, so he finally spoke. Looking around his office while gesturing with his hands he said, "Billy, do you remember the first time you were in this office, and you asked me which of these was my favourite?" I looked at the various framed photographs and memorabilia around his office, particularly the one over his left shoulder on the wall behind him. The one he had just hung up, the framed photograph of me.

I just nodded but said nothing and let him continue. There was no stopping him now, anyway. He stood up; he was walking around now, looking proudly at his collection on the walls. "Billy, the thing is, some of these...." He paused, then continued. "Some of these are just make believe, made up for Hollywood and all that nonsense, but some are genuine heroes; people who have done or are doing exceptional things, Billy. There is one person or one hero if you like who has done so much and who has inspired others to do the same."

He paused for breath again. He was more serious now, but you could still see the excited child in him. He was still walking around his office, around his framed photographs and memorabilia as he talked. "There is one person here who is just so humble, who does good simply because he can, and not for all the praise and gratitude that comes with it."

He stopped now at the newly framed photograph. "Billy, if you look at all these pictures, there are people wearing capes and bright costumes, people in disguise, staying anonymous, but who also want to be noticed, really. You once asked me which one of these is my favourite. I'm ready to answer your question now." The framed photograph was perfectly placed on the wall, he still adjusted it slightly. He framed it with his hands now.

"This guy here has an accidental cape. This guy used a plain beige Mackintosh overcoat with the intention of not being noticed. He then wore the Mackintosh overcoat while doing incredible good deeds out there. All anonymously. This guy does good for goods' sake, not for attention, Billy, and that's why this is my favourite. The anonymous inspirational Billy MacMann, better known as Mack Man, or The Man With The Mackintosh Overcoat."

So much for getting a level-headed handle on things. I wondered if I had misjudged Austin. Was he really buying into all of this? Not even that. It was like he was encouraging it all now. I was a bit angry if the truth be known, and I let him know. I stood up; I was still wearing my overcoat; I buttoned it up as I talked.

"I'm disappointed Austin. I'd have thought that you would have had a bit more sense about this, or at least been more sensitive." He was back sitting at his desk, still smiling, and looking smug. I continued. "You of all people know I didn't want any of this, Austin. In fact, I came here today hoping you would help put a stop to all this nonsense. Now we have this rubbish." I pointed to the framed photograph of me on his wall. I turned to the door and went to leave.

"Wait, Billy, just give me a minute, please." I stopped at the door and turned around to face him.

"Austin, I'm just an ordinary Joe who had a bit of luck on the lottery and decided to share it around, that's all. None of this nonsense is real. You know that, surely." I pointed to all his framed photographs again. He stood up now.

"Billy, sometimes it's the people no one imagines anything of, who do things no one can imagine."

He was right. No one, least of all me, could have imagined all the good things that were happening, never mind that it was because of an ordinary Joe, an ordinary Billy.

"Austin, you are just as responsible for all of this as I am; maybe even more so. I just put the money forward." He was still standing at his desk. "If you think about it, Austin, you have a Mackintosh overcoat, too. Maybe it's you. Maybe you are the Mack Man, maybe you are The Man With The Mackintosh overcoat." He shook his head and smiled. I continued. "Actually, the more I think about it. Austin Goodman; or Good Man! Has a ring to it, don't you think?" He laughed now.

"It does have a ring to it, I suppose. You like to use the phrase kick back, Billy. I'm one of the kick backs really, or even a sidekick if you like. Sidekick has a ring to it too, don't you think?" He sat down again. I was still standing at the door.

"Billy, I was getting disillusioned with this city. You remember the day we met. I thought that Jack Potter had won the Billion Euro. I just thought it was all so crazy, so wrong. Now I feel I'm a part of something good, something positive. I'm just glad to help Billy. I think you already know that. If the hill becomes too steep, I'm here for you. I'm here to help. For now, the important thing is to keep you anonymous for as long as we can." The broad smile was gone now; he had a more serious expression. His usual business-like expression.

"One more thing before you go, Billy…. be careful out there. For all the good you are doing, remember. Not everyone out there is good. There will be people who will be envious; there might be people that will want to drag you down." I knew what he was implying; he didn't say it out straight, so I said it.

"Austin…. you're not suggesting that I could have a nemesis out there, are you? A sidekick and now a nemesis! Really, Austin? I think you've been reading too many of your comics." He just smiled.

"I never used that word, Billy. All I'm saying is, be careful out there, watch your back, that's all."

I didn't feel any better after this meeting with Austin. Or at least he hadn't made me feel more at ease, like I had hoped. It was more like Austin was losing the plot. Maybe I was losing the plot too, losing the run of myself.

I was enjoying the secrecy of all this; I knew now that I was enjoying it too much. Every time I put on the overcoat, I felt like someone else. It wasn't a cape; it was a cover that kept me anonymous. I realised now that it was, in fact, a cover for the real kick back I was getting. The kick from being the anonymous man with the Mackintosh overcoat.

With the wedding looming, the family would be home again, and I was going to tell them all who the real Billion Euro winner was. It was time to end all this nonsense before it got out of hand, as if this hadn't happened already! It was time for me to kick back and relax; stop listening to all the nonsense. It was time for me to enjoy my riches for myself and my family.

Chapter 18

With The Remembrance Garden almost complete, I wanted to bring Claire and Jane to see it. I wanted to show it off; I was so proud of it. I couldn't tell them who was responsible. Not yet anyway. Showing it off to them was kind of the start of my process to telling them who the real winner of the Billion Euro was. I would tell them everything soon. It was only two weeks before the wedding. My family was due home in about a week. The end of the cooling-off period, the final cooling-off period.

Claire and I were meeting the manager of The Grand Hotel to finalise our wedding reception details and this gave me an opportunity to kill a few birds with the one stone, as they say. I planned a busy schedule of meetings, all at the

Grand Hotel. As you know by now, my plans never go according to plan.

I was checking the progress of the Covid Remembrance Garden, which, of course, is on the hotel grounds. Claire and Jane were joining me for this. Claire and I had our meeting with the hotel manager. Jane was joining us for this. I was giving away the last of the BMW cars. I arranged for one of the three lads to deliver the car to the hotel, so either Maurice, Larry, or Curly were joining me for this.

I also arranged to meet Austin Goodman. Claire and Jane were joining us for this. Claire and Jane hadn't met Austin yet. I would soon tell Claire and Jane about the Billion Euro and all that was associated with it; including all the help I got from Austin. Claire and Jane meeting Austin was also the start of this process.

First, I showed Claire and Jane around the remembrance garden, and we were all very impressed; It was everything I had hoped for, and more. The gardens were such a wonderful, peaceful place. Plenty of flowers and trees, there were benches to relax on, or just to sit on and reflect. I had organised memorial plaques to be put on the benches. People's names, so they would be remembered.

Angela MacMann would have her name on a bench. Benjamin would be remembered, and other front-line workers who were taken by the virus. It wasn't all going to be peaceful and quiet. There was a children's playground, a fabulous playground it was too. Everything I had organised was all coming together nicely.

After checking out the Remembrance Garden, we all went into the hotel for our meeting with the manager. I was off my guard, and I probably mixed up my persona's a little. I was supposed to be Billy showing Claire and Jane the remembrance garden, but I was acting like the man with the Mackintosh overcoat. When I walked into the hotel, I was wearing my Mackintosh overcoat proudly. I walked into the hotel as if I owned the place; I did own the place after all!

Jack Potter was there when we arrived. In fact, Jack Potter and a gang of his cronies were all having a last drinking session in the hotel. It was his last day. He was finally checking out of the hotel. I didn't realise what was unfolding around me. I should have been more tuned in.

Our meeting with the hotel manager was just a hop, skip, and a jump from Jack Potter and his cronies. Far enough away in that I wasn't worried about him recognising me, but close enough in that we could see and hear they were all enjoying themselves. Our meeting was with the manager, Darren, and Darren was in a great mood. In fact, all the hotel staff seemed to have an extra skip in their steps. Something to do with a troublesome guest finally checking out of the hotel.

Jane had arranged for Sandra to collect her after the meeting, and much to Jane's annoyance, Sandra arrived early, way too early. Sandra told Jane to take her time. She could work away in the car while she waited. She parked right beside the hotel entrance; this gave her the best viewpoint without being inside, which also gave her an opportunity to 'work away' as she put it. Jack Potter was staying at the hotel, after all.

I was giving the new BMW to Austin Goodman, even if he had somewhat lost the plot lately. I couldn't have done all the good work without him and if anyone deserved a new car, it was Austin. He didn't know about this. I planned on discreetly handing Austin the car key, with the customary 'Thank You,' message.

As things turned out, and with it being the last BMW car; Maurice, Curly, and Larry all wanted to drive it to the hotel. They had argued about it, so they all showed up at the hotel in the car. Larry won this battle and was the happy camper at the wheel driving into the hotel car park. He had two passengers in the back seat with long faces on them. Even sitting shotgun up front had been a contentious issue with them.

The brand-new BMW was parked near the hotel entrance, and next to Sandra. The lads were supposed to wait in the car park, but when they saw reporter Sandra Birch was parked nearby, they went into the hotel reception area to avoid her; They didn't want her asking them any more awkward questions.

The lads were still bickering over driving duties and were almost as loud as Jack Potter and his crew when they arrived inside. Larry had the car key; he was twirling it around on his fingers as he swaggered in. The car key holder was King. It would be someone else's turn to drive next, and this was another contentious issue with Maurice and Curly. Key to this battle was the car key.

As if to rise his sidekicks, Larry placed the car key in an empty glass at the centre of their table. I could see through the window that the new BMW parked next to Sandra had her full attention now. No doubt Sandra would have heard about a few lucky people receiving new cars from an anonymous person. Sandra would know the three lads couldn't possibly afford a new BMW car. The key to a brand-new BMW sitting in an empty glass on a table caught the attention of a few people drinking pints and cocktails.

"Anyone for more cocktails?" Was the shout from Jack Potter. An enormous cheer and a clink of glasses from his gang of cronies followed this. The thing is, there was a cocktail of events gradually unfolding around me.

So, now we had Jack Potter and his cronies' drinking pints and cocktails. Close to them, the three lads bickering, and a bit further along I was with Claire, Jane, and hotel manager Darren. Jane was bored with our meeting, so she joined the three lads at their table. Jane, joining the three lads, didn't go unnoticed by her mother in the car park.

Claire was all business-like, giving instructions to Darren. We had been through this for our cancelled wedding last year, so Claire was a bit of an expert now. I wasn't bored, but I kind of let Claire and Darren at it. I began to take more interest in what else was happening, the cocktail of events unfolding.

There was a large electronic screen above the reception desk. Jack Potter was arguing with a member of staff. He wanted the horse racing channel to be put on because he had a 'few bob on a few horses.' It wasn't a television, and this was wearily explained to Jack by the member of staff. It was an electronic notice board for hotel information and events.

Claire and I knew we were lucky to be having our wedding reception in our hotel of choice and on the date we wanted. We knew we got the date because of a cancellation. We didn't know that the couple who cancelled were Jack and Peggy Potter. It was Darren who pointed this out now. All the hotel staff were relieved to be seeing the back of Jack Potter. They were also delighted that his wedding reception had also been cancelled at the hotel.

Darren was explaining to us, step by step, how everything would go on our big day. The bride and groom would arrive at the hotel. A red carpet would be laid out and we would meet our guests for a champagne reception. All lovely and romantic. Darren was almost as excited as we were.

Darren, being a bit of a showman, took a remote control, or gadget of some sort, out of his pocket. He pressed a few buttons; and hey presto! The electronic notice board above the reception desk had changed. It flashed a new notice on the screen which Darren said would be displayed on our wedding day. The notice had the date of our wedding and, surrounded by tacky, or romantic, hearts and flowers. 'Congratulations and Best Wishes on your Wedding Day; Jack and Peggy Potter'

An embarrassed Darren apologised profusely and quickly pressed a few more buttons on his gadget, drum roll, and hey presto again; He updated the message to 'Congratulations and Best Wishes on your Wedding Day; Billy and Claire MacMann.'

All lovely and gave us both goose bumps, if I'm honest. It wasn't the horse racing, but Jack saw it. I saw him turn to look in our direction when he heard Claire's gasp of excitement at seeing the screen. He turned to look at Jane and Larry when they let out a cheer. The other two at the

table with the long faces hadn't flinched. They both still had
their eyes fixed on the car key in the glass on their table.

This was also the same moment a member of staff
arrived with Jack Potter's hotel bill for checking out. Jacks'
mood had suddenly changed. He looked puzzled now. His
eyes were still transfixed on the electronic notice board.
Without even looking at his hotel bill, Jack handed the
member of staff his credit card without saying a word.

Darren seemed to love the sound of his own voice; he'd
have kept us all day if we let him. I thought I'd be late
meeting Austin. Everything about Austin was efficiency and
professionalism, so I knew he would arrive shortly for our
meeting.

Darren ended the meeting; In fact, he ended it abruptly.
The member of staff who had presented Jack Potter with his
hotel bill had come over and whispered something in
Darren's ear. I didn't hear all that was whispered, but it was
something to do with a refused credit card. Darren was
suddenly very pale looking. He apologised to us; he had, in
his own words, 'a more pressing matter to deal with.'

Jack Potter was looking directly at where Claire and I
were seated now; he had an uneasy look about him. Jack and
his cronies all had pints and cocktails in front of them. The
cronies were all in great form, but not Jack. Jack looked
confused. I was feeling uneasy myself now. I could almost

see the cogs going around in his head. Was Jack figuring things out? Or was he annoyed that we had taken his cancelled wedding date?

The reception desk was suddenly very busy. Darren was there along with a few other hotel busy bodies. They all looked nervous and if Jack Potter was staring uneasily at me and Claire, Darren was staring uneasily at Jack, not that Jack had noticed or would even care.

This is when Sandra's curiosity got the better of her. Sandra slipped into the hotel reception area quietly. No doubt she had noticed from outside that Jane looked too comfortable sitting with what she would describe as 'three gurriers.' She stood almost unnoticed near the entrance. I noticed her, of course.

Jack was still staring in our direction. Even Claire noticed and said, "Billy, why is Jack Potter staring at us? He's giving me the creeps." He was a good thirty feet away. Jane and the lads, along with a few other guests, were seated between Jack and us. I felt uncomfortable. I had a feeling something was going to happen. Something was going to kick off.

With all this unfolding, Jane suddenly decided that this would be a great opportunity to get that photo with Jack Potter. She had missed the opportunity when her cousins were home. It would be a great addition to her TikTok page and to show off to her American cousins.

Seeing Jack standing on his own, Jane seized the moment. She suddenly stood up and walked over to him. "Jackpot, can I get a photo with you, please?" I was watching nervously, as was Sandra. Surprisingly, Jack didn't mind when Jane approached him. In fact, he looked delighted.

"Sure, what the heck? Everyone wants a photo taken with Jackpot." I suppose he was grateful to be getting a bit of positive attention. Larry did the honours and took the photograph. Jacks' mood seemed to have lightened a little now. Delighted with her photo, Jane excitedly made her way back to her table gushing,

"Thank you, Mr Potter, thank you, thank you." Equally delighted with the attention, Jack shouted back to Jane but for everyone to hear.

"Jackpot, the name's Jackpot and you can take my photo anytime."

Jane looked chuffed as she sat down, but this was when she noticed her Mother standing at the hotel entrance. Jane didn't acknowledge her, at least not formally. Jane just gave Sandra the dreaded teenage stare. Sandra was also getting looks from a few people drinking pints and cocktails; these were more dagger like than teenage stares, same thing, really.

Jack was still throwing the odd glance over in my direction. I realised that if he had recognised who I was, things could go astray very quickly, especially now with Sandra here. There was suddenly a tense atmosphere in the hotel. I felt even more worried about how events were unfolding. It was getting particularly intense amongst the busybodies at the reception desk.

Another car arrived outside. It was Austin, right on time for our meeting. I got my phone out and dialled his number before he came inside. I could see Austin answer his phone through the windows of the hotel. I briefly explained the situation unfolding inside.

Austin was calm. He thought for a few seconds without answering me. We were looking at each other now; he could see me from his car. His gaze was darting around the reception area. He was checking where everyone was seated inside.

"I'm on my way, Billy." He said calmly, and then added. "When I walk inside, don't acknowledge me; act as if you don't know me." Before I could answer, he hung up the phone. I watched anxiously from my seat as Austin got out of his car. He put on his Mackintosh overcoat; he calmly buttoned it up; he put on a face mask and brushed himself down. He opened the boot of his car and took out a hat. He put the hat on and pulled it firmly in place.

He walked to the front door of the Hotel. I watched as he paused outside, preparing to enter. He would have seen Sandra just inside the door, but with her back to him. He'd see and hear Jack Potter with his cronies taking up two tables, which were full of pints and cocktails. Jane sitting with the three lads a little further on, a few other guests, and further on again, Claire and I, who were due to meet him.

I watched as Austin took a deep breath and went to push the door to enter, but he suddenly stopped. He'd noticed a manager was now approaching Jack Potter. Austin waited outside and watched through the window. The manager was Darren, and Darren had the unenviable task of telling Jack Potter that his credit card had been refused. He welcomed Darren with a shout of, "Another one looking for a photograph with Jackpot, form an orderly queue, folks," he quipped, much to the amusement, or bemusement, of his cronies.

I watched anxiously as Darren nervously whispered the bad news in Jack Potter's ear. Jack was incensed and immediately jumped to his feet. His chair fell behind him and glasses of beer and cocktails were scattered noisily on his table.

"Don't you know who I am?" He roared. He was waving his arms around violently. Darren wisely backed away, out of Jack's reach. "I'm Jackpot! How fucking dare you; now go check that again."

Some of Jack's pals laughed, and this just incensed him even more. He was off on one of his rants so anything could happen, and everyone was fair game when Jack was in this mood.

Jane was a bit too close to the action for my liking. I did not need to worry, though. Sensing danger, Maurice, Curly, and Larry were on their feet before Jack's chair had hit the floor. To their credit, they had instinctively formed a protective wall between Jane and the now rabid Jack Potter.

Jack then spun around suddenly to face me and Claire; he was still a fair distance away from where we were seated. "I believe congratulations are in order. Aren't you the lucky couple getting married? And on the twenty-seventh of March too." He paused briefly, then repeated the words, emphasising them now. "The twenty-seventh of March!"

His eyes were darting around the reception area now. He was looking for a waiter, but all the staff were nervously gathered behind the reception desk. He shouted over at them, "Champagne! Get us champagne, champagne for everyone. We're celebrating over here. It's on Jackpot, put it on my fucking bill."

All eyes were on the unpredictable Jack Potter. His friend Macker was on his feet now and he moved closer to

Jack, but out of swinging distance. Jack turned around to face the staff at reception again and shouted, more aggressively this time, "Where is our fucking Champagne? Don't you know who I am?"

Jack had his back to me and Claire now. He picked up a half full pint of beer from the scattered glasses on his table. He took a gulp from the glass. Still with his back to us, and in a calmer voice, he said, "I used to have a Mackintosh overcoat just like the one you're wearing, pal." He turned to face me now.

I didn't say a word. I wasn't sure if he was teasing me or if he was just reminiscing about his overcoat. Jack was looking straight at me now. "How much would you have to pay for an overcoat like that, pal?" I didn't have time to answer him. I wouldn't know what to say. Austin Goodman walked into the reception area at this point. Sandra almost fell over with shock when she realised a man with a Mackintosh overcoat had just walked past her. She had her phone out instantly.

"Get your ass here now, Michael. I think I've found him. He's right here. I'm sure it's him. It must be."

Austin walked briskly in Jack Potter's direction, as if he was going to speak to him, but he stopped suddenly a few feet away. Austin tipped the peak of his hat with his hand and nodded at Jack, as if to say hello but without speaking.

He then turned on his heels and walked back the way he came, past a now panicking Sandra and out the front door again.

This seemed to confuse Jack, in fact, it confused everyone. It felt like everything was happening in slow motion now. I turned to see how Claire was reacting to all of this. She looked bewildered and whispered,

"Billy, was that who I think it was? Was that the Mackintosh man?..... Or the Mack Man?.... Whatever they call him." I sat down beside her. I wasn't sure what to make of what had just happened.

"Claire, that was...." I paused before continuing. "That was, Good Man.... Austin Goodman, the man we are supposed to be meeting."

The hotel staff at reception were whispering amongst themselves. They were distracted. If all of us seemed to move in slow motion, not Jack and his cronies. It was Macker who took charge. He grabbed Jack Potter and led the way to the hotel exit while shouting,

"Drink up lads! The party is over!" In a flash, they were all on their way out the door, but not without finishing their drinks. Pints and cocktails were necked in one go, their glasses were emptied or brought with them as they made their escape.

At first, I thought they were running after Austin and I was concerned for him, but Austin's car was already gone from the car park. They weren't running after Austin; they were doing a runner. With Jack's credit card being refused, Macker had taken advantage of the confusion and got Jack and the gang out of the hotel.

There was chaos out in the car park. It was everyone for themselves, and everyone knew if they didn't get a space in a car, they would get left behind. Cars took off towards the car park exit before car doors were even closed, but the cars all ground to a halt suddenly. Michael had arrived at this point and his car was blocking the narrow exit.

Michael froze with fright when he saw them all approaching. Before he could react, four burly men had jumped out of one car and were running towards him, cursing. They just got a grip of Michael's car and pushed it out of the way as if it was a shopping trolley.

The hotel was a lot quieter with them gone; everyone was in shock, especially the hotel staff. I'm not sure which was more terrifying for Michael, the four burly men pushing his car out of their way, or the look and curses he got from Sandra when she realised he had missed photographing the alleged man with a Mackintosh overcoat.... or Mack Man..... Whatever they call me.

There was something else. Not only did Jack and his pals empty their pint and cocktail glasses when they left. There was another empty glass in the middle of a table. The car key was gone, and so was the BMW car.

I never heard whether Jack Potter won any money on the horse racing that day; he got a bit of luck though. Someone anonymously paid his hotel bill. I did own the place after all!

Chapter 19

The day I collected the lottery jackpot, I had used the Mackintosh overcoat as a disguise, to stay anonymous. Now the overcoat was one of the main things that could expose me, make me famous even. I was determined to stay anonymous, but I still wore my Mackintosh overcoat. I believed it was bringing me good luck. It felt like everything I did since I got the overcoat had turned to gold.

I thought back to the day I met Jack Potter, when he had the overcoat and the good luck he had with it. He was lucky to escape from that terminator guy, Damo, when he put the overcoat on first. He even got his five million Euro when he had the overcoat. Jack may well have lost the five million Euro, but that was after he handed the overcoat to me.

Austin Goodman had the overcoat briefly that first time we met, and I mixed up our overcoats, he had the overcoat, my overcoat, for a couple of minutes and even his luck changed for the better. For all the good work he has been doing, it has to be said; Austin was lucky himself to meet me. Even the three lads have had a lot of luck, things are going better for them since they mischievously took the overcoat that same night I met Austin.

I only set out to help a few people and thank a few people. Things had accelerated way beyond my dreams, beyond my control. I never imagined all of this would happen. I did not know my good deeds would be copied around the world. The good work would carry on, regardless. Austin would make sure of that. He was working his wonders. He was a man on a mission.

So much was happening independently now. I may have inadvertently lit a few fuses. I did not know things would kick off the way they did. There were so many positive kick backs. I believe Austin Goodman deserves most of the credit. Meeting Austin Goodman kicked things off. He was the greatest kick back of them all.

Austin would have you believe that Mack Man is a legend, or a superhero even. I don't like to use Austin's phrase 'Superhero,' at least not in my case. Austin might have all those photos in his office, including mine now, but I knew now who the real hero was.

Austin may call himself a sidekick or a kick back. He might even be 'Good Man' as I had jokingly called him. Or maybe everyone has been looking for the wrong man with a Mackintosh overcoat. When Austin walked into The Grand Hotel to cause confusion, maybe Sandra was right; maybe it was, in fact, 'the man with the Mackintosh overcoat' who walked past her. Maybe it was the real 'Mack Man.'

I felt protected when I wore my Mackintosh overcoat. Maybe it was bringing me good luck, or maybe I just imagined it was. I was sure of one thing. I was riding my luck, and the good luck would run out sooner rather than later. I was also dragging out the cooling-off periods. I was using them as excuses.

It was just one week before our wedding day. My family was due home again. Austin had given me so much good advice. Now it was time to seek different advice or inspiration. It was time I visited my Mother's grave again. This visit to my mother's grave and events that followed felt like I had come full circle from the last time, back in January, when I went looking for advice or inspiration.

As I tidied the grave, I noticed there was a funeral going on not too far from where I was. I recognised one of the mourners. It was my school pal Kevin Quinn; I had heard he was doing well now. Austin was still giving Kevin helpful advice and keeping me informed.

It was a private funeral, so I didn't want to impose. Kevin had seen me, though; he followed me to the car park. I was about to get in my car when I heard a familiar shout behind me. "Are you still driving that poxy taxi?" Kevin wasn't just doing well now with his business; he looked well too. I could see the stress had lifted from him. The funeral was for an elderly relative of his.

Kevin didn't know all the good things I had done for him. He didn't know that I was his landlord giving him free rent, or that I had arranged for the vouchers to be spent in his restaurant. He did remember that I kick started it all by getting a friend of mine to advise him. This friend of mine was Austin. Kevin wanted to thank me, but not even that. He wanted to give something back.

He was looking to expand his business, maybe even open another restaurant. Kevin offered to help me now, give me a job, or as he put it, "A chance to give up the poxy taxi." I was delighted things had turned around for Kevin. I told him I would let him know about his job offer.

As I went to leave the car park, my poxy taxi wouldn't start. What was I supposed to do? I decided to get the bus home. I stood at the bus stop thinking about the last time I had been on a bus. It was the day I went into Lottery head office with my simple plan. What a journey I'd been on since then.

A BMW drove past me but then stopped suddenly with a screech of the brakes. The car reversed back beside me, erratically. I had to step out of the way. It was Emma, one of my mother's carers, and she was driving one of the cars I had given away. I don't think I ever saw a smile as wide. Emma was driving a shiny new car, but the car faded to the background behind that smile.

"Billy? I thought it was you. Jump in. I owe you a lift." So, I jumped into the passenger seat. I had to play dumb, of course.

"Wow Emma, look at you and your new car. Did you win the lottery?" Emma laughed.

"I feel like I did, Billy." She looked around her car proudly before continuing. "Let's just say I got it from a secret admirer." She laughed again. She cranked the gear stick loudly as she continued talking. She struggled, but finally found the correct gear and took off, narrowly missing my parked broken-down poxy taxi. I quickly put on my seat belt as Emma talked. "Now, Billy, when I say a secret admirer, I mean someone who admires the work I do. Can you believe it? A brand-new BMW car!" She was delighted with herself, and rightly so. She deserved it as far as I was concerned; she had been so good to my mother.

I got the full story as we whizzed along. How the car was delivered by three cheeky chaps, and she thought the car was stolen when she saw them, but the paperwork was all in order. Her smile seemed as wide as the road. It wasn't just the new car; Emma was chuffed that her good work was appreciated.

There were a few occasions on our journey where I regretted not getting the bus. With all Emma's talk, she tended to forget to look at the road ahead of her, and I had to remind her more than once. Apparently, there were loads of new cars given away. Emma would nearly have me believe that everyone she worked with got a new car.

"Even Doctor O'Sullivan got one! As if Doctor O'Sullivan needed another BMW car." She exclaimed. I had a different view to this. I knew that Doctor O'Sullivan deserved a reward for helping my mother.

I got my poxy taxi back the next day. Trainee mechanics Maurice, Curly, and Larry sorted it out for me. If I'm honest, with all the new cars around. This is when I realised it was time for me now, me and my family. All this money and I was still driving a beat-up poxy taxi.

So many people had benefited from my good fortune, but there were so many secrets I was keeping from Claire. I had bought her dream house, and she didn't even know it. I could buy myself and Claire any car we wanted. Heck, I could buy her parents and her sister any car they wanted. Maybe I should order another batch of new cars and give them all away, all except one, or two.

I'm not sure if the BMW cars, and I mean me not having one, were playing on my mind, because everywhere I went the next few days, there seemed to be a BMW car just around the corner. When I say around the corner, I mean literally. The car, or cars, seemed to be just ahead of me or just behind me, but I could never see who the driver was. There were at least the eight that I had bought out there on the streets, plus countless others. I felt like I was being teased for not having a new car myself.

Chapter 20

I had a busy week ahead. We all had. Things kicked off with two airport runs. The two Catherine's arrived on Tuesday with Ciaran and Zoe. The Chicago crew burst on the scene next day. The MacMann's were all home for the wedding. Claire had family arriving too, so things were getting hectic. My family was staying in The Grand Hotel again, and everyone was buzzing for the big day.

I was pretty much all set for the wedding. I had two things to do. I had a last fitting for the wedding suits, and I had to tell Claire about the Billion Euro. The suit fitting could be done now that everyone was home. Claire seemed to have lots to do. We barely saw each other with all the running around.

With all this running around and hullabaloo going on, Claire and I arranged to go out for a meal, just the two of us, a last date on our own before we got married. I also saw it as an opportunity to tell Claire my secret. I wanted to tell her first, and I had to tell her before we got married.

Yet again, I had a simple plan and yet again my plans didn't go according to plan. At our meal, our date, I was going to tell my wife-to-be that we were Billionaires. Let her in on the secret. We could then tell the rest of our families. We, as in Claire and me, would then give them life changing amounts of money.

We, as in all the boys, had the last suit fitting. I was meeting Claire afterwards for our date. I was nervous about telling Claire but excited, too. It was all going to be good. I would deflect a lot of the good stuff in Austin's direction. I knew that I should have told her earlier, much earlier, but I would blame Claire for that. The cooling-off period was her idea, after all.

My Best Man Martin had organised the wedding suits, so it was his gig, and I just went with the flow. Brad, or Flash as he liked to be called, was going to be my Groomsman on the big day. The wedding suit crew consisted of me, Martin, Brad, Ciaran, Austin, Claire's Father Gerry, and the three numbskulls: Curly, Larry, and Maurice.

You might ask why the three numbskulls were going to wear wedding suits. The three lads were on driving duty from now until the wedding day. We suited them up because they were chauffeuring family and friends around. I had also taken a bit of a shine to them. As Bruce said, they were good lads, most of the time. I had given into temptation and bought a new batch of BMW cars, six more in fact. I just couldn't resist.

I wasn't giving all the cars away. The numskulls didn't know it yet, but when the wedding was over, they could keep a car each. They earned them; They were a great help to me. I was giving Claire's father Gerry a car, too. The other two cars? His and hers, or mine and hers. I had parked them in the driveway of Claire's dream house. Claire still didn't know about the house. I would reveal everything on our date.

The three drivers drove us all to the suit fitting. Bizarrely, or coincidentally; Martin had ordered our suits from the same shop where Jack Potter had taken the now famous Mackintosh overcoat back on the day I first met him. I kind of felt guilty when I walked into the shop because I was sure Jack didn't pay for the overcoat. I might have paid Jack five million Euro for it, but I still wondered if the shop assistant would recognise it as stolen.

The mannequin at the front of the shop was still there, back in one piece again since the skirmish with Jack Potter. It even had a new Mackintosh overcoat on for all to see. There was a bit of harmless fun and chaos at the shop as tailors measured and re-measured the crew. Brad wasn't impressed with the suits. He had hoped for one with more flash and flair and argued this point with Martin, much to the bemusement of everyone. While this was going on, I was drawn towards the mannequin with the Mackintosh overcoat at the door.

I thought back to the day Jack Potter took the Mackintosh overcoat from the same mannequin and all the amazing things that had happened since. Martin caught me staring at the mannequin. "Snap out of it, Billy. We have work to do here." He walked over beside me, and realising the mannequin was wearing the same Mackintosh overcoat as me, he took a fit of laughing.

"Well, well, well; Billy. That's your twin right there!" He could barely control himself with his laughing. He indicated for the shop manager to come over. "We're going to need another suit. Turns out Billy here has a long-lost twin brother." They both enjoyed the joke. Martin whispered something in the manager's ear and they both laughed. I'm sure it was at my expense. I would be privy to the joke later.

With everyone measured for a suit, we were all set for the big day. I was all set for my date with Claire. No more secrets. It's not every day you get to tell your wife-to-be that they are one of the wealthiest people in Ireland. I was nervous all the same.

The restaurant was quiet when we arrived. Claire looked fabulous; I felt like the luckiest man on the planet, and maybe I was. Except something didn't feel right. It was Claire; she looked fabulous, but she was in an unusual mood. I had this unbelievably important thing to tell her, but she just seemed all giddy, distracted even. I took a deep breath before I began.

"Claire," I said it in a serious tone, which caught her attention, but only briefly. "Claire, I have something I need to tell you." I was expecting her to, well I don't know what I expected. Maybe I thought she would at least focus on our conversation, but no, Claire seemed to be somewhere else. I continued.

"Claire, you know the way everyone has been wondering who really won that Billion Euro jackpot?" She just nodded casually. She was distracted and kept looking over my shoulder. She was barely listening to me.

"Sorry, Billy, what were you saying?" I was getting a bit annoyed, but I stayed calm. This was all going to be good, I told myself. So, I continued.

"Claire; I was saying about the Billion Euro jackpot winner, and how everyone has been wondering who it is." She was still distracted; her attention was elsewhere. I couldn't see what Claire could see over my shoulder.

Martin was at the door behind me. They were all there, the wedding suit crew. They weren't wearing the wedding suits, but they all had something else from the suit shop. They were all wearing matching Mackintosh overcoats. Identical to the one my long-lost mannequin twin had been wearing, identical to the one I was wearing.

A bit disillusioned with Claire's lack of interest in what I was trying to tell her, I went to look over my shoulder, to see what was distracting her so much. Claire grabbed my hand in hers before I had a chance.

"Yes, Billy, you mean the man with the Mackintosh overcoat?. Like your overcoat, I suppose." I was getting a bit deflated.

"Well…. yes Claire…. kind of I suppose." I took another deep breath, more in exasperation this time. "When you put it like that. What if I told you I'm that man, Claire? What if I told you I am the man with the Mackintosh overcoat?"

Then it happened. The quiet restaurant was suddenly noisy. I found myself surrounded by men in Mackintosh overcoats, MacMann's even. Best man Martin had arranged a surprise stag party for me. Claire knew all about it. Her job was to get me to the restaurant and to keep me distracted.

To everyone's delight and with roars of approval, I was bundled into one of the BMW cars outside. Claire, who had been so giddy and distracted, had a different expression now.

"Mind him, Martin; keep him safe now. No stupid carry on out of you." Martin had a cheeky glint in his eye.

"Oh, don't you worry Claire, I'll look after him all right." Claire knew too well how immature Martin could be, so she turned her attention to the three young drivers.

"Larry, Curly, Maurice; you're Billy's minders for the evening. Mind him, get him home safely." I didn't get a chance to say anything else to Claire; it was Martin's gig again.

The bits I remember, we had a great night. We went on a pub crawl; the three lads took Claire's instructions firmly on board. I had three minders for the night. It must have been some sight at the various pubs having all of us walk in wearing identical Mackintosh overcoats. We were like a 'Man with the Mackintosh overcoat,' or 'Mack Man' themed stag party. It was all harmless fun for most of the night.

When I say most of the night, I mean right until the end, and our final pub visit. Of all the bars in all this town; We ended up at The Crock of Gold for our last drink, the old 'one for the ditch' as they say. We weren't the best for wear at this stage.

We all thundered into the pub loudly and excitedly, and if I'm honest, it probably resembled the scene when Jack Potter and his cronies had barged into the same pub way back when I was there with Claire. I was going to tell Claire about the Billion Euro that day. This time it was me and my stag crew who were causing a scene.

I hadn't noticed him at first, but Jack Potter was there. He was a lone figure this time. He was at the end of the bar counter, close to where Claire and I had been sitting that day. Jack wasn't sitting. He was leaning against the bar counter. The way he was leaning forward, it looked like he was holding the bar counter up. In reality, it was the bar counter that was holding him up.

The sight of a drunken mob bursting in and all of us wearing Mackintosh overcoats would have been a sight, especially for the lone figure at the end of the bar. If we weren't the best for wear, Jack Potter was in bad shape. I only realised he was there when there was a shout from where he was standing or wobbling uneasily.

"Hey, mister…!" He wasn't addressing anyone in particular; he was just shouting in our direction. He was unsteady on his feet and swaying side to side. He had his pint in one hand and took his other hand off the bar counter to point at us when he shouted. "Hey mister, you with the overcoat. I'm talking to you! You never did tell me how much you'd pay for an overcoat like that."

Without the bar counter holding him up, Jack suddenly stumbled forward, almost crashing to the floor. Miraculously, he somehow stayed on his feet and didn't spill a drop from his pint glass. Years of experience, I suspect.

His friend Macker appeared from the shadows. He'd been there in the background, as he always was, looking out for Jack. He helped Jack steady himself. The unappreciative Jack swung out at Macker, but he was ready for it and ducked out of the way. Years of experience again.

Missing his target, the momentum carried Jack forward, but Macker ducked back in and caught him before he fell to the ground. "Fuck off! I'm all right." Pint still in hand and swaying side to side, Jack staggered over in our direction. The closer he got, the more confused he seemed to get.

He addressed Brad first, with a pointed finger. "Hey, I'm gonna need…. I'm gonna…." He stopped mid-sentence in confusion, and then turned his pointed finger to Martin, who had his hands out front ready to catch him if he fell forward. It was a mean feat how Jack was still upright and not spilling a drop from his pint.

I stood behind him, ready to catch him if he fell backwards. The confused Jack spun around to face me, his finger still pointing all this time. "Stand fucking still, will ye? Don't you know who I am?" Pointing his finger at himself now, he exclaimed loudly. "I'm Jackpot!"

Surrounded by men in Mackintosh overcoats, the confused Jack turned left, then right. He didn't know who to address with his pointed finger. "I'm gonna need that fucking overcoat back, pal; the deal is off, it's off I tell ye."

Macker stepped in and led Jack away from us. Jack didn't fight him off this time; he seemed relieved to see someone who wasn't wearing a Mackintosh overcoat. Jack was still ranting as he was led away. "I'm not going until I get my bleedin' overcoat back."

The overcoat crew saw the funny side of it all, but we took our overcoats off. They were all piled in a corner in case Jack Potter came back and caused another scene. Groomsman Brad was struggling; we all were. Brad, being only eighteen years old, is too young to drink alcohol back home in America. In Ireland he's allowed to drink, and he took full advantage, but he overindulged. We all did. The pile of Mackintosh overcoats made a comfy bed for him to sleep it off.

The event didn't dampen our night; it played on my mind though. I wasn't sure what to make of Jack Potter's mind set. Did he know who I was? What did he mean by 'the deal is off?' And why does he want the Mackintosh overcoat back? I felt responsible for him somehow. Sensing my unease, Austin walked over beside me. I just sighed.

"What can we do for him, Austin? There's no point in giving him more money. He'll blow it all gambling again." Austin put his arm around my shoulder.

"You're right, Billy, and you owe that man nothing, but if you're determined to help him, I have an idea that might work." We both sat down. I was uneasy on my own feet. Austin continued. "What if Jack got a regular income?" I interrupted him.

"You mean like…. like, give him a job?" Austin laughed.

"No, no, that wouldn't work. Let's say…." Austin paused for a few seconds in thought, then continued. "Do you remember that money you borrowed from him, Billy?" I laughed this time.

"The money I borrowed?" I said it too loud. Austin shushed me, then whispered,

"Billy, if you can't remember, then neither can Jack. If you're that concerned, maybe you need to pay back the money neither of you can remember you borrowed. Pay it back on a weekly basis. What do you think? Maybe a couple of hundred every week?" What Austin said made sense, and I wanted to help Jack.

"Sounds like a plan Austin, the thing is, I probably borrowed more than you remember and guys like Jack Potter charge crazy interest rates, too. It's going to cost me…. four hundred a week…. I probably need to pay him in instalments too. Maybe two hundred twice a week? What do you think? Can you organise that, Austin?" He shook his head in disbelief.

"Consider it done, Billy."

Chapter 21

When I woke up, my head was throbbing. I had a vague memory of the three lads helping me into the house. As I slowly pieced things together, I'm pretty sure that when I arrived home, I drunkenly told Claire that I won the Billion Euro and that I was Mack Man. I had made a total fool of myself.

Claire was beside me now, bright eyed and wide awake. I could barely even open my eyes. The light just made my hangover worse. "Good morning, Billy MacMann, or Mack Man, as you called yourself last night." She was laughing when she said this. "Looking at the state you're in this morning, you obviously had a great time last night." She laughed again. I wasn't going to get any sympathy from her. I just grunted.

She was in great form. "Billy, can you believe it? We're getting married tomorrow!" I tried to share her excitement but could only manage another grunt. When I woke for a second time, I was on my own. I didn't feel much better but managed to drag myself out of the bed. Claire had left a note for me.

'Hope you're feeling better, Billy,' followed by a few smiley faces. 'I've things to do and I'm meeting Jane in town. I'll phone you later. XX. The future Mrs Mack Man.' Yep, that's how she spelled it, followed by several more smiley faces.

It was the day before our wedding, and I still hadn't told Claire we were Billionaires. Well, technically I had told her twice, but she wasn't listening the first time and the second time she thought it was the drink talking, and it was, in fairness.

I was feeling rough but managed to struggle down the stairs. I needed to get my head straight, and I had to meet Claire. I had to tell her everything. I phoned her and she was with Jane; I still didn't get any sympathy from her. They had lots to do but agreed to meet me for a coffee. It was good Jane was with her. I decided I would tell them both, tell them everything.

I left the house, habitually making sure the coast was clear. It wasn't. 'Be nice, Billy,' I told myself. It was my lucky day, though. Mrs Fogarty didn't come running across the road to me. She was on the way out of her house, in a hurry. She shouted over to me without stopping. "I haven't got time to talk today, Billy. I'm getting my hair done, you know, for the big day tomorrow. I'll see you and Claire at the church."

She was gone, scurrying down the road. Almost immediately, Mr Fogarty was at his front door. He was looking up and down the road, making sure the coast was clear. Seeing me, he whispered loudly,

"Is she gone, Billy?"

"It's all clear, Mr Fogarty." I said, while signalling thumbs up. He let out a sigh of relief, put his hat on, and went scurrying down the road in the opposite direction to his wife. He suddenly stopped, turned around, and walked across the road to me. He put his hand out, we shook hands.

"Best of luck tomorrow, Billy. Best wishes to you and Claire. Your mother would be so proud, God rest her." He paused briefly before continuing. He still had a firm grip on my hand. "She was a special lady, Billy, a very special lady." I thanked him. He released his grip; he was looking up and down the road nervously. "I better go before the dragon comes back." He had a chuckle to himself. "See you tomorrow." He scurried off again, holding his hat on with one hand while looking over his shoulder anxiously.

He was right, my mother would be so proud. She always loved family gatherings. I was proud of her, too. She was a special person. It was my mother that helped influence all the good deeds that had happened, that were still happening.

I got a parking spot not too far from where we were meeting. I was on my way to tell my wife-to-be, and my daughter, that I was the real winner of the Billion Euro jackpot and, by definition, The Man With The Mackintosh Overcoat. I grabbed my overcoat and buttoned it up as I walked along.

As I was buttoning up, I realised that it wasn't my overcoat that I had. It was the same as mine, but this was a brand-new overcoat. The overcoats must have got mixed up at the stag party. I thought back to the last time I mixed up my overcoat. That was when I met Austin Goodman and what a good man he turned out to be.

I took the overcoat off and folded it over my arm. I didn't really mind. I was about to tell Claire and Jane everything. I was getting married to the fantastic Claire, and we were having a new baby soon. I was going to enjoy my riches now. We all were. I could see her and Jane further up the road, laden with shopping bags and both all smiles when they saw me. Claire managed to free one of her hands from her shopping and gave me an almighty wave.

As I waved back, I was thinking to myself; 'Am I the luckiest man in the world right now?' I was getting married to the love of my life and I had Jane, a wonderful daughter. I wouldn't swap them for all the money in the world.

And that's when it hit me. I never saw it coming and had no time to react. Jack Potter came around the corner and knocked me off my feet. Again! He wasn't running or being chased this time. He was driving a stolen BMW car and this time I didn't get back up on my feet.

The overcoat flayed behind me, cape like, as I was flung through the air. I landed with a thud and a crack. Jack lost control of the BMW and crashed into a parked car, which just happened to be my poxy taxi. I could feel myself drifting unconscious.

Bruce was suddenly standing above me. "Stay still Billy, don't move. You need to stay still. I couldn't answer him. I couldn't get the words out. I couldn't move. The Duke started licking my face. I could hear Jane and Claire screaming hysterically from further down the road.

In the corner of my eye, I could see Jack Potter squeezing himself out of the BMW car, where he had been wedged between the air bag and the seat. Not a bit concerned about my wellbeing, Jack made a move for the Mackintosh overcoat, which was now resting on the pavement beside me. The Duke positioned himself protectively between me and the advancing Jack Potter.

The normally placid Duke snarled at Jack Potter. This stopped him from advancing further. Jack Potter snarled back at The Duke. "Get outa my fuckin way, ye flea-bitten mongrel." And that's when it hit him. He never saw it coming. A punch from Bruce knocked the shocked Jack Potter flying backwards and out for the count.

When I woke up, my head was throbbing. In fact, I was sore all over. My immediate thoughts were what about the wedding? But it was the day after our wedding day. Our wedding had to be cancelled, again.

Naturally, Claire and everyone were just relieved that I was going to be okay. I had a concussion, a few broken ribs, and a dislocated shoulder. I was beat up, physically and mentally just beat up now. It could have been worse, I was told. The doctor even told me I was lucky. It didn't make me feel any better, though.

I had to stay in the hospital for a few more days. There were another couple of airport runs due. I wasn't fit to do them. The three lads were on driving duty. Family all called in to see me and say their goodbyes. The goodbyes were emotional. Big sister Catherine was in to say her goodbye first.

"You're so lucky Billy. We are all so lucky to still have you. Thanks be to God you're going to be okay. Our Mum was looking out for you, Billy." Catherine gave me a big hug, almost cracking a couple more of my ribs. She turned to Claire and gave her an equally big hug. "Mind him, Claire, take care of our Billy. We'll all be home again to see the new baby, and for the…." She paused. She had tears in her eyes. We all had. "You'll have to reschedule the wedding, won't you? When you're ready." She then turned to me. "Billy, you have to mind Claire now. Do you hear me? Take care of Claire. She needs you more than ever, Billy." It was time for Catherine to go. "Just mind each other, mind yourselves. I love you all so much. Take care." And reluctantly, Catherine was gone.

Martin was next in and tried to be as positive as he could.

"We'll get you two married yet, Billy and Claire. We go again!" He paused, not knowing what to say next, and probably looking at our less than enthusiastic expressions, before continuing. "Next time…. next time you lot are all coming to Chicago. We're going to get you two married, and we're getting you married American style."

Martin turned to Claire, who was smiling but had tears in her eyes. "Girls like Claire won't hang around, Billy. We go again; third time lucky and all that. You two…. you two just need a bit of good luck, that's all. You just need to get a lucky break." I just smiled, half-heartedly.

"We will go again, Martin, maybe after the baby is born. Who knows?" And just like that; my family was all gone again. I still hadn't told them about the Billion Euro and still hadn't given them their share. I had to tell Claire first, and I intended on telling her, finally telling her, as soon as I got out of the hospital and home.

When Jack Potter woke up, his head would have been throbbing, too. Jack was arrested, but he was back on the streets again in no time while he awaited his trial. I haven't decided if I will press charges. Maybe a stint in jail will do him good. A bit of a cooling-off period might be just what he needs.

I didn't have the Mackintosh overcoat now. I got an unexpected visitor in hospital. Maurice and Jane brought Bruce in to see me. Bruce was minding the Mackintosh overcoat for me again. He had picked it up after the ambulance took me away. He wanted to give it back and insisted on handing it to me in person.

Bruce asked Jane and Maurice to leave the room so we could be on our own. As Jane and Maurice left, I noticed they looked very cosy together. I wasn't sure, but they might have been holding hands as they closed the door behind them.

Bruce got straight down to business. "Billy, people call me Bruce, but my name is Boru, my real name is Boru O'Brien. Nothing happens in this town without Boru O'Brien hearing about it. I hear and know about everything. Everything! I wanted to thank you Billy, thank you for everything you've done; And I mean Everything!" He emphasised the word everything.

I went to speak, but he raised his hand to hush me. "Let me finish Billy…. I want you to know I'm known for my big talk and bigger stories, but I'm a man of honour, Billy MacMann, and I can keep a secret. You can trust me on that." The way he was looking at me, I knew what he meant. I knew what secret he was referring to. He also meant what he said. He held the overcoat out for me to take. I was reluctant to take it off him.

"Bruce… or Boru, can I call you Boru?" He nodded in agreement. "Boru, I want you to keep that overcoat. I'm stepping back for a while, taking time for my family. I've no doubt that you have heard that I have a few sets of eyes and ears on the streets." He just smiled.

"I told you they were good lads, Billy, and for all my talk, no words could tell you how much I appreciate what you've done for them all."

"Boru, I need someone else out there. Someone…. someone who sees and hears everything that happens in this town. I need someone to let me know when something needs to be done, when something needs to be kick started; if you know what I mean." He didn't say a word. He just nodded in agreement and folded the overcoat. He took a carrier bag out of his pocket, and carefully put the overcoat inside.

"I have to go, Billy; The Duke is waiting for me outside." Just before he got to the door, I called him back.

"One more thing before you go, Boru." He turned around to face me. "You say nothing happens in this town without you hearing about it." He puffed his chest out proudly.

"Yes, that's what I said, Billy, and I'll tell you something else; If I don't hear about it, then it probably didn't happen."

"Boru…. can you tell me?" I paused for a couple of seconds to get the wording straight in my head. "That nephew of yours…. Maurice, he is a good lad, a great lad in fact…... Tell me Boru, have you heard anything?" He just looked at me blankly, waiting for me to finish the question. I continued, "Have you heard?…. Is there anything going on between your Maurice and my Jane?" He had a wry smile.

"You're right Billy; I did say nothing happens without me hearing about it. Do you remember what else I said?" I looked at him blankly. I was trying to think what he meant. He continued. "I also said I could keep a secret, Billy." With that, he turned around and walked out the door.

Bruce might say he knows everything that happens in this town, and I have no doubt he can keep a secret. I can keep a secret too. What Bruce doesn't know is that the original Mackintosh overcoat is still out there somewhere. Someone from my stag crew has the overcoat now; they mightn't even know that they have it. I wasn't really bothered. It's just an overcoat. Right? I couldn't help but wonder, though. With my accident, and the wedding being cancelled; Had my luck changed now?

It might be just an overcoat but, if I'm honest, it kind of did bother me. I wondered where the overcoat was. I had a feeling my original Mackintosh overcoat would show up again.

Chapter 22

Almost one week after the accident, if you can call it an accident, the doctor discharged me from hospital. Austin was with me when Claire and Jane arrived to take me home. I was feeling a lot better, physically anyway. I was going home. I was finally telling Claire and Jane everything. Austin knew my plan; he was still bewildered as to how Claire and Jane hadn't figured it out themselves.

If Claire or Jane had ever asked me, I would have told them the truth. They never said anything, never asked. I suspect Jane saw it as an imaginary character, like in her TikTok video and all the other fun videos that it inspired. I did try to tell Claire a couple of times without success. I imagine Claire would believe that the winner was entitled to their privacy, to stay anonymous.

There were people who suspected Austin Goodman won the Billion Euro and was the man with the Mackintosh overcoat. Maybe Claire and Jane suspected he was. So much of the good work wouldn't have happened without Austin. As far as I was concerned, Austin was, in fact, 'The man with the Mackintosh overcoat.'

Austin still wore his Mackintosh overcoat. It was time for me to step back, let Austin continue the good work. Metaphorically hang up the Mackintosh overcoat, I suppose. I didn't even have an overcoat to hang up now. I had given mine to Bruce.

Maurice was on driving duty. My poxy taxi was poxed for good, thanks to Jack Potter. No big deal. After I tell Claire I will bring her to our new house, Claire's dream house, and our new cars. After all that had happened, Claire and Jane were just delighted to get me out of hospital and home. I was still a bit beat up, but I was okay. I was looking forward to just getting home myself.

I was ready to go. I could see Maurice from my window. He was parked near the hospital entrance. He had a trigger spray and cloth in his hands and was patrolling the car. The car looked immaculate, but Maurice was like a trigger-happy gunslinger from the Wild West, looking for trouble and daring dust to settle on the car so he could shoot it off with his gun spray and cloth.

I couldn't resist fishing for information with Jane. "So, Jane…. I see Maurice is waiting outside…. Did Maurice give you a lift here?" Claire jumped to Jane's defence straight away.

"Don't mind him, Jane; tell him to mind his own business." Jane, well able to look after herself, Jane weighed in defensively.

"Well, if you must know, Dad! Maurice didn't bring me here. Mum dropped me off; she was coming this way on her way to work." This should have set off alarm bells with me, but it didn't, until my phone rang. It was Maurice. I could still see him from the window, trigger spray in hand, still looking for trouble, and he found trouble.

"Head's up, Mr MacMann. There's a bit of trouble brewing out here. Nosey Bitch…. I…. I mean Mrs Birch; Mrs Birch is at the front door here and it looks like she's on official business, if you know what I mean." Maurice calling me Mr MacMann was very formal for him, but I let it go. I would have let the nosey bitch comment go, too. It was a fair description.

I didn't answer him. The alarm bells were ringing for me now. I turned to Jane.

"Jane, is your mother collecting you, too?" Getting annoyed with me being nosey now, she snapped back.

"You know fine well that Maurice is waiting outside to bring you, me, and Claire to your house. We're just friends, Dad, good friends…. sort of." Maurice was still on the line; he sensed my unease.

"Give me two minutes, Mr MacMann. I'll get on the blower and sort it." He ended the call. I could still see him outside. He was back on his phone, or 'the blower' as he put it. Sorting it, I suppose, whatever he meant by that.

Sandra Birch was one of the most popular and unpopular reporters in Dublin. She never got to reveal the answer to her question. I was wondering now. Had she finally figured it out? Austin and Bruce had figured it out. I looked at Claire and Jane. I was sure they hadn't figured it out. I was determined that when they hear; it would be from me, not from a nosey reporter on the street, even if she was Jane's Mother.

There was a chance that Sandra was outside because Austin was here. There was the incident at The Grand Hotel recently. Austin had also seen Sandra, or one of her colleagues, following him occasionally. He used to get a laugh from it. If Austin suspected he was being followed, he would take his overcoat off and hold it over his shoulder, like in the photograph.

When Jack Potter was arrested after knocking me down, it was a big news story. My name was not mentioned in the news, Austin had seen to that. Sandra knew it was me. In fact, in fairness to her, she even sent me a nice get well soon message.

Sandra would want a sensational headline with another sensational photograph to go with it, regardless of the consequences for anyone else. Wouldn't she just ask me to my face? I was wondering if that was Sandra's plan; that would be her sensational story, and photograph. All this was going through my head in the two minutes it took Maurice to 'sort it' and get back on the 'blower' to me.

"Ok, it's sorted. They are on the way. Send Mr Goodman down first. Let's see if there is a reaction. If nothing happens, send Janey and Claire down. You'll need to go out the back door; Curly and Larry will meet you there." I didn't know what to say. What did he mean by 'they are on the way?' And who did he think he was, calling Jane Janey?

Everything seemed so rushed suddenly. I got myself ready to go. I wasn't sure how I'd explain things to Claire and Jane. I looked at Austin; He was already buttoning up his overcoat. He said a brief goodbye, said he would phone me, and off he went. Part one of Maurice's plan was in operation.

Jane was over by the window now, sneaking a little wave to Maurice. I went over to have a look, much to Jane's annoyance. I was just watching to see if there would be a reaction to Austin walking out the front door. I was kind of hoping there would be. Austin got past the door with little fuss. I couldn't see Sandra from where I was. I watched as Austin crossed the road. He phoned me immediately.

"This is it Billy, it looks like she's here for you, not even that. Jack Potter is down here too. It has all the makings of an ambush, Billy, and it looks like you're the target." I thought for a few seconds. My plans never work out.

"We'll stick to the plan, Austin, Maurice's plan." Part two of Maurice's plan was already beginning, and this is when I found out what he meant by 'when they arrive.' Jane saw them first.

"Oh gosh, there's something happening outside; what are all those people doing here? And look, that's Bruce and The Duke out in front of them all."

There must have been about thirty of them. Bruce had rounded up a posse of his friends and associates. It was time to return a favour, or favours, another kick back.

Bruce was standing front and centre with his Mackintosh overcoat on. He was like the town Sheriff, and maybe he is the Sheriff. All he was missing was a badge. 'They' were all wearing Mackintosh overcoats or makeshift overcoats of some description. Some of them were holding sleeping bags over their shoulders, mimicking the photo of me when I left Lottery head office with the overcoat flaying, cape like. Jane opened the window to get a better view, phoning Maurice while she did so.

"Moe, what's happening down there? Is everything ok?" With a better view Jane recognised a couple of other people. "Is that Mum down there? And Jack Potter? What are they doing here?"

Claire was over at the window now. She turned and looked at me with a confused expression but didn't say anything. It looked to me like she was stringing things together in her head. With the window open, we could hear a bit of what was going on outside. Bruce stepped forward to face Sandra Birch. His head held high, he proudly announced.

"I am the man with the Mackintosh overcoat. I am Mack Man." Another of the posse stepped forward.

"No, it's me; I'm the man with the Mackintosh overcoat." It pretty much became a free for all then, with all of them claiming to be 'Mack Man' or 'the man with the Mackintosh overcoat.' It was all bizarre. It seemed to take Sandra by surprise; she looked shocked. Jack Potter stepped forward to face the crowd. He got a look from Bruce and quickly stepped back behind Sandra. Using Sandra as a shield, he meekly declared.

"I'm Jackpot! Get the hell out of here, the lot of ye." This got a great laugh from the posse. More determined now, they all shouted back in a mixture of declarations. Some now claiming they were 'Jackpot' and others claiming to be 'Mack Man' or 'the man with the Mackintosh overcoat.'

It was time for the next part of Maurice's plan. Jane and Claire were fascinated with what was going on outside. With Jack Potter out there, I had an excuse now.

"It's time to go home," I said. "You two need to go on ahead. I don't want to face Jack Potter yet, I'm not ready for it. Curly and Larry are collecting me out the back; I'll explain everything when we get home, everything!" I paused, exasperated by everything. "We all just need to get home."

Jane couldn't wait to get down and see all the action outside. Claire was hesitant. She wanted to stay and go with me, make sure I was okay. "Please, trust me, Claire; I'll explain when we get home. I'll.... I'll explain everything, Claire." She was reluctant to leave. They were both at the door now. Claire looked confused and had a quizzical expression.

"Billy, what do you mean, you'll explain everything?" Jane was getting impatient and tried to hurry Claire.

"Let's go, Claire! We're missing it all. We need to get down there." I went over and gave Claire a hug.

"Claire, it's all good, I promise. We'll all be home in about fifteen minutes." Jane had Claire by the hand and wouldn't let go; she was tugging at her, trying to hurry things along. Claire looked confused.

"Billy, are all those people down there because of you for some reason?" I looked her in the eye.

"Yes, Claire. Everybody is down there because of me. I'll explain everything. I'll see you…. I'll see you at home in about fifteen minutes." Unable to resist the pulling of her hand from Jane, they both left. Jane excitedly, Claire reluctantly.

I watched from the window as Jane and Claire walked outside. Claire was looking at the crowd as she walked past and then looked back up at me. She still had that quizzical expression on her face. Jane marched straight up to her mother. It looked like she was having a right go at her.

"Why are you here, Mum? And with Jack Potter! After what he did to my Dad!" Jane turned her attention to Jack now. "You! Jackpot! More like Jackass! I'll get The Duke to sort you out!"

Claire seemed oblivious to what was going on, she was still looking back at me quizzically. She grabbed Jane by the hand this time and dragged her towards the car, and a nervous looking Maurice.

Jane gave Maurice a big hug and a kiss. I'm sure it was more to annoy her mother than for Maurice's benefit. It was time for me to go. I instinctively went to grab my Mackintosh overcoat. Of course, I didn't have one now. Bruce was outside wearing my Mackintosh overcoat, or at least he was wearing a Mackintosh overcoat. I wondered where the original one had ended up. I just needed to get home now.

It was time for the final part of Maurice's plan. So far, so good, I was thinking. I made my escape towards the back of the hospital, the back door. I could see Curly and Larry waiting for me; they had their own trigger sprays in hand and were giving their immaculate BMW car the once over.

It felt like the day I left the Lottery head office again, except this time, I was leaving by the back door and Jack Potter, Sandra, and the crowd were all at the front. I wondered what would have happened if I left by the back door that day. Michael wouldn't have gotten that photograph. I didn't need an overcoat as a disguise now.

I went to push the door open but suddenly stopped. 'Where was Michael?' I asked myself. Michael and Sandra worked as a team. I didn't see Michael at the front of the hospital. There was mayhem going on, but Austin didn't say

Michael was there. I pushed the door open halfway but didn't step outside.

"Michael, I know you're there. Michael, I just need fifteen more minutes. I just want to go home and tell Claire and Jane myself. Is that too much to ask?" Nobody answered. I paused, took a deep breath, then stepped outside. And there he was, camera in hand.

The two lads with trigger sprays realised what was happening and ran in our direction. I raised my hand towards them in a stop motion. They both stopped, startled, not knowing what to do. Michael and I were just as startled. We were just staring at each other, not knowing what to do. Michael had his camera ready. His phone started ringing. He looked at his phone, smiled, then said,

"Do you mind if I take this, Billy?" He answered his phone. He barely had time to say 'hello.' I could hear the voice. It was Sandra.

"Michael, you idiot! You're wasting your time there. Get your ass back here now. Jane and Claire are in the car. It looks like they are waiting for him here. I'm sure he'll be coming out any second now and God help you if you're not here when Billy comes out." Michael simply replied,

"I'm on the way." He ended the call, smiled wryly and then looked at me and said. "Billy, I was just wondering. Did you know a cousin of mine has a car just like that one over there?" Michael pointed to the BMW car parked across the road. I didn't answer him. He continued. "Billy, a cousin of mine does a lot of good work for visually impaired people. A new car was delivered to him recently, as a gesture of thanks from someone anonymous. There was a generous cash donation for his charity too…. Billy, you wouldn't happen to know anything about this, would you?"

I didn't answer him. I just stood there, motionless. We could hear the commotion from the front of the building. Bruce and his posse were causing a racket, still claiming to be 'Mack Man' and 'the man with the Mackintosh overcoat.'

"I better go, Billy, or there will be hell to pay. Best of luck to you. Keep the good work going. I'll tell Jane and Claire you'll see them at home in about fifteen minutes." With that, Michael turned around and made his way towards Sandra at the front of the Hospital, hurriedly now. I knew fine well who Michael was referring to. I had also received another positive kick back.

I arrived home before Claire and Jane. It was nice and quiet, gave me a chance to gather my thoughts after the rush of events. Finally, I could explain everything to Claire and Jane, if they hadn't figured it out themselves. No more excuses, no more distractions. I felt like a weight was going to be lifted from my shoulders. Maybe Martin was right. When everything was out in the open, Claire and I could set a new wedding date. Bring everyone to Chicago and get married there. Third time lucky and all like he said.

I looked out the window and saw the BMW car arrive outside. We were all home. My phone rang. It was in my pocket; I ignored it. No more distractions. It rings out but almost immediately the landline rings; I ignore that too. Looking out the window, Maurice is helping Jane out of the car and he's a bit over friendly. Maybe I need to have a word in his 'shell like.'

My phones have stopped ringing, but I see Claire answer her phone as she walks towards the front door. She catches me looking out and gives me a cheerful wave. Jane and Maurice catch me looking too. They both give me a sheepish wave.

Claire is talking to someone on her phone as she walks to the front door. She suddenly stops walking. I don't know who she's talking to, but her mood is more serious looking. She looks at me through the window again and her mood suddenly changes again. She's hyper excited now. "I don't believe it!" she exclaims in a high-pitched voice. She gets Jane and Maurice's attention and says something to them.

I open the front door to let them in. I'm ready to... well, I wasn't sure what I was ready for or what I was going to say. They all run in the open door and past me towards the television. Claire puts the television on.

"Billy, have you been watching the news?" I turn around and look at them, confused. "It's all over the news. Martin has been trying to phone you; they have named the Mega Millions Jackpot winner."

The news on television is live, but there's no Sandra Birch in sight. In fact, it's a live news feed from Chicago. The jackpot winner is holding one of those giant cheques. It's a cheque for One Billion Dollars. It's difficult to see who it is with all the high jinks, and people clinking champagne glasses.

There is a new Mega Millions Jackpot winner. The winner is wearing a Mackintosh overcoat, just like mine. In fact, it is my Mackintosh overcoat! Button up your overcoats. It looks like this jackpot winner is not staying anonymous. He's out front and centre, loving all the attention. It's my nephew, Brad! There's a new man with a Mackintosh overcoat. Wait until the world gets a load of Billionaire Brad…. Flash Mack Man!

Jane and Maurice are bouncing around the room excitedly, but I'm looking at Claire. She's just staring at the television with a shocked expression. Jane bursts out with, "Way to go, Flash! One Billion Dollars…. and isn't that your Mackintosh overcoat he's wearing, Dad?" I don't answer. I'm still looking at Claire. She suddenly turns around to face me. I can't tell whether she is in shock or angry,

"Billy MacMann," she says. Then whispers it to herself a couple of times while staring at me, "Billy MacMann…. Billy MacMann…. Mack Man! It's you Billy! You are the Mackintosh man!"

She is in shock, but she is angry too by the look of her. She has her hands on her hips now, and dagger eyes. I back away from her while holding my hands out front, defensively, trying to calm her down.

"Claire…. I tried to tell you. I…. I will explain everything, Claire. Right now you need…. how should I put it? Claire, you need to take a cooling-off period!"